The King of Kings

**Book Three of the Immortal Kindred
Series**

A.D. Brazeau

The King of Kings
Book Three of the Immortal Kindred Series
Copyright © 2019 A.D. Brazeau
All rights reserved.

ISBN: (ebook) 978-1-949931-08-2
Print: 978-1-953335-52-4

Inkspell Publishing
207 Moonglow Circle #101
Murrells Inlet, SC 29576

Edited By Audrey Bobak
Cover art By Maria Spada

DEDICATION

For Brian and Quinn, and my parents, Marilyn and Craig.

A.D. BRAZEAU

CHAPTER ONE

The air inside the tomb was stale, fetid. Light from scattered torches cast an eerie glow. The few people inside seemed illuminated by the orange of the flames. My mother, Isis made flesh, stood near an altar with her advisor, Meskhenet, their heads close together, voices barely audible.

Fear wound its way up my legs, threatening to take hold of my core. This sort of emotion was unknown to me. However, any feeling of terror must be kept to myself. Mother could not tolerate weakness, especially in me, the son she called the king of kings.

They discussed their next move. Moves were something we seemed to be out of, locked as we were in what was meant to one day be my mother's place of rest. There was only a handful of us here; me, Mother, Meskhenet, and two loyal servants. We would all walk gladly toward the afterlife for her.

Mother's shoulders moved up and down with a sigh. Looking toward me, she beckoned me to her with one outstretched hand. In an instant, I was at her side, grasping her warm, golden brown hand in mine, much paler by comparison. Physically, I was Roman through and through, the genes of my father being strong. Mother said the gods had touched me as a babe, turning my hair the color of the sun, as bright as Ra himself.

I knew Mother had to be tired, but no one would've been able to tell by looking at her. She possessed all the regality, all the self-possession of a true queen. She was a self-contained unit, my mother; strong, smart, and more politically savvy than any man. Her inner self was hers alone. My little sister and brothers made a game once to guess how Mother was feeling. I judged the competition, handing the winner a plateful of honeyed dates. To see her come to this was a blow to everyone who loved her.

She pulled me into a hug, the beads of her net dress biting into my skin. I inhaled her scent of spice and aromatic oils, uniquely my mother and one I would never forget. Almost as soon as she embraced me, she pushed me away, squaring her shoulders and looking me levelly in the eyes.

"Caesarion, I must prepare for what lies ahead. It is my time, my destiny to ascend to the afterlife." I began to interrupt her, but she silenced me with a hand. "I have no fear of death, and neither will you. My fear is not in dying, but in what that monster will do to me if I am captured. I will not find out. I am Cleopatra, Pharaoh, Queen of Upper and Lower Egypt, Isis made flesh, prisoner of no man. You, my son, will leave here. Meskhenet and I have a plan. You will not give any trouble. You will carry on as the living god you are. One day, you will come into your own. Until that day, you will remain safe out of Octavian's clutches. There's no one he fears more than you. You may never rule Egypt or Rome, but you are special, Caesarion, touched by the gods, and your day will come."

I fell to my knees, pressing the back of my mother's hand to my lips, squeezing my eyes shut to prevent the tears from falling. My mother's will was iron. There was no use in trying to convince her to let me stay.

"Take this." My mother slid her gold snake bracelet from her upper arm and passed it to me. She wasn't a sentimental person and I wasn't either, but this bracelet was a symbol of her. She always wore it, in fact, I teethed on it as a child. I slipped the gift onto my wrist. "There is no more time. Meskhenet will tell you the plan as you go. Stay safe, my son, and above all else, stay alive. I will see you again, one day."

I almost thought I detected a crack in her voice, but before I knew it, she'd turned away. I wanted to tell her I loved her, but Meskhenet was throwing a blanket over my shoulders and thrusting a bag into my hands. "This way, my prince. We must go, now," he said with much urgency.

"Goodbye, Mother," I said to Cleopatra's back. She held her hand up in farewell.

I could hear the Romans outside, barely audible through the thick stone. They were trying to gain access to the tomb. It would take some time, but I knew they would eventually succeed. I steeled myself as the son of Cleopatra and Julius Caesar, determined to follow Meskhenet through a narrow doorway.

"How will we get out?" I asked the back of Meskhenet's dark head. I noticed for the first time his once black hair was beginning to whiten. When had that happened? In the chaos of the last few months, there was much that had gone unnoticed.

He may have been older, but Meskhenet walked with the speed of the young. "There is a tunnel that will take us about a mile into the desert and out a secret passageway."

"Surely Octavian will be scouring the country for me. He won't allow us to get far," I reasoned. I had as much, if not more claim to Rome than he had. Although, I would never want it. Egypt was where my true soul resided. But he wouldn't want me to rule here either. I was nothing but a threat to him.

"We have sent a decoy out ahead to Berenice. That ploy should buy us all the time we need. The imposter will negotiate through messengers with Octavian. Then possibly return based on the outcome. If return is possible, we will be able to go home. You will take the place of the imposter and claim your throne."

Berenice was a seaport. The Romans would be watching all seaports like hawks. I didn't see my return as likely, and I didn't think my mother did either. I thought of my mother and her exceptional mind. A mind which would be lost now, for all time. A lump threatened to form in my throat. I swallowed it down.

With the speed in which we traveled down the hot, dusty passageway, it wasn't long before we reached the hidden entrance. I wouldn't have been surprised to see Octavian, astride his warhorse, torch in hand, waiting for us as we emerged. When Meskhenet pushed open the small stone door and we surfaced into the nothingness of the vast desert, I breathed a sigh of relief. There was no one, only miles and miles of endless sand.

"Where will we go?" I asked as I pushed the slab closed behind me. "And why did Mother not try to escape this way?"

"We will go west, where we will wait in a village. When enough time has passed, we will see. We can be sure of nothing any longer. And as to the queen, she alone knows her mind. I would think you would understand this, having been her son for seventeen years."

I understood Meskhenet, as I understood Mother. She did nothing that was not first expertly calculated, her moves more skillful than a Senet player.

Crossing the desert was a hardship of the first degree. How we managed it was all due to Meskhenet. He kept us covered during the day and managed to find water when we needed it, almost as if by magic. He was a mystic, after all. Food was harder to come by. We endured several days together without solid sustenance. Mirage after mirage played on the horizon, only to be endlessly replaced by a new illusion.

By the time we arrived on the northwest coast of Africa, we were ghosts of our former selves, but we were alive. Meskhenet and I were taken in by a small village, where we were happy to stay put for the time being. Meskhenet assisted the local healer and I helped tend the animals. Life was pleasant, calm. I did my best to put the events in Alexandria behind me.

By winter, Meskhenet had grown so visibly old and weak, I knew he couldn't last much longer. There was word that Roman soldiers were once again searching for the son of Caesar and Cleopatra. Octavian had been informed that the boy he'd executed in Egypt wasn't the real Caesarion. How he found out, I never knew. Likely, we were betrayed by someone close. I knew the boy was being well rewarded in the afterlife for his loyalty and sacrifice.

On a silent, cold evening, I entered the hut I shared with Meskhenet. "I've brought you some broth and I order you to eat it," I said, putting the bowl into his shaking hands.

He pressed the bowl back toward me, sinking lower into his bed. "I need no more nourishment for my physical body. It will be cast off this night."

"You're just tired. You need to eat and to rest." I felt a burning rise in the back of my throat. What would I do alone?

"No, my boy. It is time. There are things I must say to you." He paused, swallowing with difficulty, his eyes watery, not from tears but old age. I sat on the stool next to him, grasping his hand. It was clear he didn't have long, whether my heart would accept it or not. "I can't see an obvious way for you to ever return. You are vulnerable as you are. Octavian has grown too powerful, with tentacles reaching every which way. You are a lost man, without an army to back you."

"I don't care. I don't even want to rule anymore." I didn't want the throne. I wanted a simple, peaceful life no longer controlled by machinations for political gain. The months we spent in the village were the only quiet ones I had ever known.

He held up his hand. "This matters not. He will still pursue you. You must be made invulnerable."

"How do you suggest I do that? I would have thought

my mother invulnerable, but even she is gone," I said with sadness in my voice. My gaze found the bracelet, entwined on my wrist.

"There may be a way. Cleopatra may punish me for it in the afterlife, but I will take the chance if it means you will be safe, always. You are too special, and you must continue."

I looked at him, perplexed, as he went on. "There is an old legend, passed down to me. It tells of a woman, a woman who has learned to trick death. She lives forever and is powerful. She was sent to live on the island of Kovos. You will go there and find this woman. For me…you must."

"A woman who lives forever? It isn't possible, Meskhenet."

"It is. You will go there, and you will see. Give your word to a dying man."

I looked down at the blanket covering the withering body of my friend. I felt this was foolish, but what harm could it do to go? I would have to move on at some point, and this island seemed as good a starting point as any. "I give you my word."

He smiled warmly. "Good. I need your word in one more thing. Prepare my body in the Egyptian way."

I swore I would. It was a peaceful transition. I sat with my friend, holding his hand, as he slowly passed out of this world and into the next.

It took me several years, but I did eventually keep my word. I knew if I didn't leave the village, once and for all, I never would. In the spring of my twenty-fifth year, I was on a barge, heading toward an uncertain future.

The day we arrived on the mysterious island, with the sun at its midpoint, I was ready to start anew. Sweat trickled down the side of my face as I shouldered my bag, walking off the barge. A breeze would have been appreciated, but the air was oddly still. I didn't feel there was any point in wasting time. I would do my best to find this phantom woman, then I could move on.

I followed Meskhenet's instructions, beginning my journey to the center of the small island. I had no money, so I was forced to go on foot. The deeper I moved inland, the thicker the jungle became. The cacophony of birds, insects, and skittering reptiles was deafening. This place didn't seem like it belonged, somehow. I had the impression it was in the wrong part of the world. By the time I arrived at the island's center, the sun was setting.

Twilight winked out before I could find shelter, giving way to total darkness. There was no moon, no stars to be seen through the dense jungle trees overhead. It was when I began hearing things move around me that I realized I had made a horrible mistake. I should've waited until morning to come here.

A rustling to my left, followed by a low, predatory growl, almost stopped my heart from beating. I froze as a dark shape with glowing eyes moved slowly in front of me. It was a panther, and she was hungry. I could barely see the outline of her sleek body. She had a pungent, wild smell. There was nothing I could do. As we stood in the middle of the path, eyes locked on each other, another rustling from the opposite side won the panther's attention.

What happened next was a blur. One moment, the panther was there, looking over her shoulder. The next, it was gone. I stared wildly, but I could see nothing. I could, however, hear. What I heard were the sounds of an animal being torn apart; a cry from the beast, bones snapping, ligaments tearing. Then, nothing. I stood petrified, frozen to my spot.

"I've never seen hair that color before." A high, childlike voice startled me out of my skin. She was so close, I could smell the meat on her breath.

"Who's there?" I whispered.

"My name is Layla. Who are you?" asked the voice in the darkness. This was her, I knew it. I didn't know how I knew, but I did.

"I'm Caesarion Ptolemy, son of Queen Cleopatra and

Julius Caesar," I said firmly and with pride. "I've come to find you, Layla." There was no point in hiding my identity from a woman who could take down a panther with her bare hands.

I jumped a little when small fingers took hold of mine. "Come this way, Caesarion Ptolemy."

Surrounded by darkness, Layla led me through the jungle. How she could see was a mystery to me. Eventually, we came to a great cave. A break in the foliage overhead allowed light from the night sky to illuminate the opening.

Dampness permeated the mouth of the cave. I could smell the water, the moisture seeping from the stone. I still couldn't see much of anything in the darkness. She led me further and further into the deep recesses of the rock. Fear began to take hold of me like a fever.

She must have sensed my discomfort because in her small voice, she said, "Do not be afraid, my boy."

"I'm not afraid," I said, more to convince myself than her.

She said nothing more until I could see a soft light glowing up ahead. "Our destination," she said. "You will be glad to rest."

It would have been ridiculous to deny her reasoning. I felt like I could sleep for days. I was also hungry. I didn't want to be rude and ask her if she planned on feeding me. There was some bread along with a skein of water in my bag, so that would do for now anyway.

As we neared the light, my eyes readjusted. I was finally able to make out the stone that surrounded us and the figure of the woman who led me. I noticed she was less of a woman than she seemed. She was slight, her figure immature. Looking down at her wrist, I noticed how delicately boned it was. Obviously, this being didn't need bulk. Her power came from within.

"Here we are," she said, releasing my hand.

The space, lit by two torches, reminded me of my mother's boudoir, albeit dirtier. Rugs that had once been of the best quality covered the floor. They were now threadbare and stained with dark splotches. Pillows of all shapes and sizes were strewn about. These would have made the space seem luxurious if not for their filthy condition. Dozens of scarves had been tucked into cracks in the rock walls as a sort of decoration.

"What do you think?" asked Layla, who spun around the center of the room with her arms flung out.

"It's very lovely," I answered, feeling something was wrong, off. The smile hovering on this creature's lips looked almost mad. Perhaps it was a trick of the light. Her smile frightened me more than her single-handed takedown of the panther.

"Thank you for taking me in," I began. "How old are you, Layla? You look awfully young to be here all alone."

She laughed a high-pitched child's laugh. She couldn't be more than fifteen. "I can take care of myself. Didn't you witness my strength? You with your powerful body were helpless. Besides, it's you who have come looking for my help."

I suppose I had, but I wasn't sure what I expected or wanted from this girl. Meskhenet said she was immortal. Other than taking down the feline beast and seeing in the dark, she didn't look like my idea of an immortal godlike creature. She reminded me of my little sister with tightly curled, dark hair, and light brown skin.

Selene, my half-sister, had been the spitting image of our mother. A pang I thought long-buried ached in my chest. I heard the children had been sent to Rome, paraded in chains, and then given to Roman families. I didn't know if they lived or died.

"I'm not sure if I require help any longer. I feel I am safe now. I only wanted to fulfill a promise." Truth be told, I was beginning to feel panicked in the space. I needed fresh air. It was close and pungent in here.

"No, it is more than that. You cannot hide your thoughts from me. You believe the legend of me in your heart, no matter what your brain may try to make you think. You are special, Caesarion. There will never be another with your unique bloodline. Your mother was right when she said you were touched by the gods. You can rule greatly, if you so choose." She paused, sinking down on the pillows. "And I'm sorry to tell you. They are dead. You are all that remains of the mighty queen." Any trace of her crazy smile had vanished, and she appeared almost normal now.

"How can you know all that?" I demanded, anger flashing through my skull.

"I can hear what you're thinking as clearly as if you spoke the words aloud. Sit with me, Caesarion." She gestured to the pillows across from her. "Do you want to know more about me? About what you could become?"

A thought dawned on me. If I were like her, I could do whatever I wanted. Never again would I be afraid. "What could I become?" My curiosity was piqued.

CHAPTER TWO

Caesarion may be who I was, but Alexandre was who I became. The name the long-ago villagers gave me stuck. Once I left the island, Alexandre became synonymous with decadence, egoism, and pleasure. I reveled in my new nature, never looking back.

After seeing Annie in the streets of Annecy, I retreated to the cabin I inhabited two centuries ago. Only a glutton for punishment would return to a place that could now hold only painful memories. Losing my head to the lover of the woman I thought was the love of my life made me question a lot about myself. I felt I deserved a little self-indulgent wallowing.

I never thought a woman would almost be the death of me. I was lucky I kept the important detail of destroying the brain from her and Annie. I never told them anything, really. My instinct was always that Mills could turn on me some day, turn on me if she found out the truth about Julien. Her love for that milksop, so disgusting and all-consuming.

I certainly failed with her and it all began the night she came to me in this cabin. Part of me was amazed it was still here. The solid structure of stone and mortar would serve me for the next few days while I tried to figure out where

Alexandre would go from here.

Never was I so struck by anyone, as I was by Millicent. She was beautiful, yes, but I saw inside her soul the night of her wedding party. She was good, truly kind at heart in a way that was rare. She had so much light and love to give. Her beauty and passion wasted on the fools around her.

I fell for her immediately. It took all of my strength not to snatch her up then and there. Millicent was too young that night for the change to be worked. I saw what eternal adolescence did to my maker; being changed so young and living so long. I would not send Millicent down the same path. I was patient and waited for her to fully mature, knowing when our moment came, we would love each other for an eternity. I had all the time in the world, after all.

Then, *he* came along as I was preparing to turn her, to make her my eternal companion. She would have loved me, I knew it, if not for him. How could I have predicted it? For her to fall so deeply in love, and with such haste, I couldn't accept it. Not when I waited so long for her. It was maddening to think of, even now. Then to think the same soul would find her over 200 years later. It was too much.

Clearly, she was not meant to be mine. I could see that now, as much as my heart still ached. What comes next was the question. Would I find myself a new love, a new family? Or hide here for time immemorial? Hiding sounded like a plan I could live with.

Although the cabin was in remarkable condition, considering its age, some of the old, wooden shutters had rotted away. I would need to make my domicile safe for daytime sleeping. I went to work without delay, chopping fresh wood to cover the windows and seal the door from the inside.

I felt like a lumberjack splitting wood in old dusty jeans and a flannel shirt. My expensive, fashionable clothes were left behind to rot, much as the wood inside the cabin. My limbs would find themselves in more casual fare for the time being. If only a damsel were to come along. She would see the bulge of biceps as I worked the ax. A little tryst against the woodpile may help my mood immeasurably.

The bed remained in usable condition, along with the small table and chairs I made myself two centuries ago. I was proud of the craftsmanship. The old feather mattress along with the ancient bedding, torn and fouled by woodland creatures, were tossed out back on a makeshift trash pile. A brand-new sleeping bag was unfurled onto the boards of the bed. Cobwebs and dust were swept away with a t-shirt from my pack. Not the luxury I was used to, but it would suffice for the soulful meditations to come.

I lit a fire, feeling almost cozy. Once the cabin was as tidy as I cared to make it, I lay down with my thoughts. I wasn't a boy who grew up camping with family, but I imagined those sorts of memories must smell like the cabin did; of campfires and pine needles.

A scent invaded my senses. I wasn't alone. The smell of fresh, human blood drew me from my reveries. This blood was innocent, and it smelled sweet like pulled taffy. My mouth started to water. Could it be my damsel, lost in the woods at night? After moving to the door, I stepped outside into the dark clearing.

Several raccoons, rummaging in my trash pile, scattered at my footsteps, leaving in their wake a musky odor. An unseen owl hooted from the treetops before taking flight.

A woman stood at the entrance to the forest, alone. I wasn't born yesterday and didn't trust this. One glance told me this was no maiden. She had come down the same path I had shown Mills so many years ago. Only it wasn't her. This woman looked dressed for the zombie apocalypse in combat boots, a black military-style sweater, and a compact black vinyl backpack she dangled from a fingertip. Around her thigh was strapped a large hunting knife, and there was a bulge in the waistband of her pants I assumed to be a gun. She was also gorgeous. Color me intrigued.

"How fun. Please tell me I can be of service," I said, raising an eyebrow and smiling at the fair-skinned, freckled beauty.

"Actually, you can." Her Irish brogue was lilting. "Can I trust you won't drain me dry?"

Well, this creature had me completely perplexed. She knew what I was, and she knew where to find me. This could either be amusing or end in disaster, for her, of course.

"I promise to be gentle…if that's what you prefer." I smiled my most wicked smile, getting nothing in return. It was dark, but the sky was brilliant with stars. I'd no doubt she could see me quite well.

"Is the inside of this hole habitable?" she asked. "This may take a while. Our *discussion* may take a while," she emphasized, remaining in place next to the trees.

I stood aside, sweeping my arm toward the door. She trotted across the clearing. Deep red hair swished as she walked. When she entered the cabin ahead of me, the soft citrus scent of orange blossoms momentarily filled my senses. I followed this mysterious woman inside, claiming a spot at the antique, wooden table.

"Please sit." I indicated the only other chair. Who could this woman be? I thought of Annie, my spy. She could probably speak the redhead's language better than I could.

My visitor's hazel gaze swept the interior of the cabin. She must have been satisfied because she flung her pack onto the table, then took a seat. She moved with intention, not grace.

We sat for a moment, regarding each other. She wasn't as young as I initially thought, around thirty-five, I estimated. Her eyes were just beginning to crinkle at the corners, and a few worry lines creased her brow. This woman had seen things. If I drained her, I could see them, too.

"You have me at a disadvantage, my dear. You seem to know more about me than I know about you. A polite lady would introduce herself." I affected an attitude of nonchalance, leaning back on two of the chair legs.

She rolled her eyes. "*My dear. Polite lady.* Let's bring it up to the twenty-first century, okay? I'm not here to ask you to be my friend, or anything else."

"Then why are you here?" This woman had succeeded in intriguing and irritating me in less than five minutes. Did everyone have to be so serious all the time? I was the one in emotional pain.

"I need your help. *We* need your help. My friend and I," she said. She sat slumped over the table, her hands in front of her. Good posture had gone the way of polite manners.

I rubbed my chin and started laughing so hard I nearly fell over in my chair. "This must be a joke. You are one hot piece of…woman, but I don't help people. The only person I help is myself. And, anyway, I'm afraid I'm not in the mood at the moment. It's been a hard couple of centuries, and I need a break from humanity. You have precisely sixty seconds to tell me your name and purpose here. You don't want to know what I'll do if you don't comply." I leveled my most serious don't-mess-with-me expression at her eyes. She didn't so much as flinch.

"You don't frighten me, Alexandre. Maybe this is your moment to change who you have been in the past. My friend at least believes you deserve another chance." She blinked her eyes slowly, rolling them to the side. She seemed to be giving a side eye to someone who wasn't even in the room.

I looked toward the empty space where she had thrown her bit of shade. "Life doesn't work that way, but maybe you haven't been around long enough to figure that out. And how do you know anything about my past? Speak plainly or leave." I now sat straight in my chair, the front legs slamming into the floor, ready to put an end to this interview.

"I've been around long enough. My name is Bria. I need your help to fight a demon. Is this plain enough for you?" Her face was as stony as a poker player.

Oh, this poor girl. It made sense to me now. She was

insane. I'd had enough of madness to last me three lifetimes. "A demon," I repeated. "Hm-hmm. I'll just show you out."

I moved to get up. Bria slammed her hand down on mine. "Stay put," she said. This woman had a lot of gall, I had to give her that.

"Child, you are beginning to make me angry. You don't want to do that. You seem to know who I am. If you know as much as you're putting on, then you know I'm not to be trifled with." I was far too fascinated by this woman to drain her. Still, she was treading on thin ice.

She moved her hand back to her side of the table. "Is that so? You're a vampire who has killed, what? A handful of people? On the scale of evil I've seen, you're around a four out of ten."

I crossed my arms in front of my chest. "A four? Hmmm. All right…Bria. I'm curious if nothing else. Spin your yarn." Why not listen to what this Irish beauty had to say? I had nothing better to do. Maybe I could turn this into the opportunity for playtime I was hoping for earlier.

"Do you have anything to drink before I begin? It was a long walk from the road." She raised her eyebrows, as if anticipating I would say yes.

I couldn't believe this woman who had disturbed my solitude was now asking for refreshment. "No." My voice sounded more bitter than I intended.

"No bother." Bria pulled her backpack into her lap. Reaching inside, she brought forth a silver flask, opened it, and tipped a healthy portion of amber liquid into her mouth. The sharp odor of alcohol wafted toward me. Wiping her lips with the back of her hand, she stifled a hiccup, then said, "I'm not a stereotype. A good slug of whiskey never hurt anyone."

I smiled, in spite of myself. I could've liked this woman under different circumstances.

"What I'm about to tell you may come as a shock."

"Do you honestly think anything a mortal could tell me would be shocking?" I was having a hard time keeping my façade placid. A shiver made its way up my arms, causing my hairs to stand on end. She had my attention. Just because I had never seen a demon didn't mean they didn't exist. The unexplainable was all around us.

"All right. I was only trying to warn you, but now I'll let loose. Your sister is the one who sent me." She paused, narrowing her eyes to penetrate mine. I wasn't used to receiving news of this kind. I didn't like it. First, I had to deal with the reincarnation of Julien, and now with someone who claimed to be the issue of Cleopatra. The world teemed with people who thought themselves of royal descent. I may have believed her story of demons, but to throw in my sister? Now, I knew this woman was nuts. Hot, but nuts.

"Look, I have a high tolerance for foolishness, sometimes it can even be a little entertaining. But, this, this is not amusing. I'm simply not in the mood." Thoughts of playtime were over. I wanted to be alone in my misery.

"Please hear me out. Selene would have come herself, had she been able. Instead, she sent me and asked me to give you something."

My teeth clenched at the name. Selene? Meaning Cleopatra Selene?

Bria reached into her backpack yet again, this time retrieving an object wrapped in a white cloth. She set the bundle in the center of the table and drew away the cover. My hand flew instinctively to my mouth. I actually believe I gasped. Me, of all people. Even the events in Savannah didn't surprise me as much as this one small bit of gold. I thought my life couldn't get any stranger. Why did drama always happen in clusters?

"The physical differences between the two of you are interesting. Other than stature, you have no traits in common I can see." Bria's gaze swept over me.

"I wholly resemble my father, albeit with lighter hair. Selene and the other children of Marc Antony took after our mother." Julius Caesar was tall, fair, and fit of body. Although I have seen him described in literature as having dark eyes, Mother always said they were light blue, like mine. I didn't remember noticing his eyes on the few occasions I was in his presence. It was his bearing one noticed.

I picked up the ring, rolling it between my thumb and middle finger. There was no mistaking it. The lapis scarab beetle was always worn on my mother's index finger of her left hand. She was very particular about certain things. Could it be real? Cleopatra Selene was alive. Not reincarnated, but alive?

Layla had been right and wrong when she told me the other children were dead. The two boys, one of them Selene's twin, disappeared into thin air, likely assassinated. However, Selene, I was later to find out, had lived until around the age of thirty-two. Exactly how and when she died was a mystery, but she survived after being taken to Rome. She became the wife of a king and had children of her own. It was a comfort to me, knowing my mother's line had continued.

"Why couldn't she come?" The sound of my voice, ragged with feeling, surprised me. So many years had passed since I last thought of the events of that time, of the people who were my real family, my blood. Something strange, a stirring, took place inside me.

"She couldn't come because only those who carry the blood of a god can hold the portal." She held up her hand, inspecting a fingernail. Bria was very adept at dropping a little crumb of information and then leaving it there to hang in the air.

Carries the blood of a god? I was used to my mother and Layla saying I had been touched by the gods, but to suggest we were gods, this was too much. I had a high capacity for bullshit but come on. I set down the ring and rubbed my hands over my face. My body was so tense, agitated, I felt I could rocket out of my seat. My muscles tightened all throughout my body.

"I have no idea what you're saying. Let's handle one revelation at a time, if you don't mind. How is she still alive?" I was going to need paper and pencil to keep track of what Bria was telling me. The air in the room grew warm. Bria's human cheeks started to take on a ruddiness to pretty effect.

"She's a vampire, like you, of course. How else could she still be alive?" She dropped this next morsel then closed her mouth again like I was the biggest idiot on earth.

"A vampire like me. Yet, she never came to me, never sent word to me? Cleopatra Selene has been alive for the last two centuries, and I've never heard from her?" This was more unbelievable by the second. Sadness and anger welled in the back of my throat like white-hot heat.

"I know you must have questions about that, but Selene is the one to answer them, not me. Your family drama is not my business. My purpose here is to tell you about Balor and enlist your help." Bria absentmindedly tapped on the table, setting my teeth on edge.

"Balor?" I squeezed my eyes shut, balling up my fists on the table.

"Balor is the god of death."

Of course, he is, I thought. I had recently lost my head and didn't feel like losing it again. Brave I was not. If there really was a god of death named Balor, I wanted nothing to do with it. When someone had *death* as part of their moniker, it was best to stay away.

A.D. BRAZEAU

CHAPTER THREE

"The god of death doesn't sound like someone I would like to meet. I'm sure you ladies can handle the situation on your own. You look quite capable." I got up, moving toward the door of my cabin. I stood, waiting for her to exit, not very patiently. "Tell my sister hello for me. She hasn't cared to see me for two thousand years, why start now?"

"You really are something, aren't you?" Bria turned her body toward me but remained seated. With a scowl and narrowed eyes, she looked at me indignantly.

"I'm a lot of things. Smart being at the top of the list. Which is why I would like you to leave now." I was ready to bodily remove this woman from my hole, as she'd called it. Verbal volleyball with a woman I didn't know from Eve was not presently on my to-do list.

She crossed her legs and leaned back in her chair, as if settling in for a long discussion. Why couldn't this person leave me in peace? "You aren't a lot of things. You're maybe two or three things, tops. Shall I tell?"

"No thanks. I'm getting hungry and it's time for you to go." How many ways could I tell someone to leave? I should've been ripping her to shreds, yet something about her held me back. It wasn't so long ago I took the life of an innocent. Taking another was easily done.

"Number one, you're selfish. Number two, arrogant, and number three… well, that seems to be all. Are you proud of your two traits? Selfishness and arrogance? Your sister and I cannot do it on our own. It pains me to no end, but we need help, specifically your help." Bria was no closer to moving from her seat.

"Why mine, specifically?" I remained with my hand on the door, wondering what it would take to find some peace. I did want her to leave but hated to admit I was interested in learning more about my sister.

"You and Selene are special, like I already said. Only those descended from gods can vanquish another god." She said this as if she was tired of explaining the situation to me. Only she hadn't explained anything. At this point, she could have written me a book and I still wouldn't understand.

I rubbed my hands over my face, truly wearying of this nonsense. "I am the son of Cleopatra and Julius Caesar. They may have declared themselves gods, but they were flesh and blood the same as you. What do I have to do to get you out of here?" My blood began to boil inside my veins, confusion addling my brain.

"You aren't technically the son of just Cleopatra and Julius Caesar."

I blinked hard. "What do you mean by *technically* and *just*?" If there was one thing I was sure of, it was my parentage.

"Selene can explain this better than I can." She sighed, picking lint off her jeans.

"Well, Selene couldn't bother to come!" I interrupted, anger now boiling over.

Bria slammed a hand down on the table and stood. "Because she's the only one who can hold the portal!" she shouted right back. "This is what I know, as explained to me by Selene; your father and her father, Marc Antony, were possessed by the god Osiris, and your mother by the goddess Isis, when you and the twins were conceived.

Unfortunately, the other twin was lost long ago." She stood there, watching me closely.

I slumped against the wall behind me. Disbelief hovered in my mind. I thought back to those long-lost centuries. All of us worshipped the gods, but my mother's focus was predominantly on Isis. She professed to be the embodiment of the goddess on Earth, claiming to be Isis many times. I always believed she meant this metaphorically. My mind kept hitting on her saying, "You have been blessed by the gods, my son. You are uniquely special." I had to wonder if she knew. She must have. I shook my head, hoping to rid my mind of these thoughts.

"I can't do this right now. I'm sorry, but I can't. I've just been through…" I trailed off my sentence, staring out into space. What was there to say to this lovely firecracker of a woman? Even if I hadn't been through hell, I didn't have it in me. I was no hero. The sooner Bria and Selene figured it out, the better. If my sister and I were descended from gods, then it stood to reason there were others like us in the world.

Bria sighed loudly, still standing next to the table. "I told her you wouldn't come."

I shut my eyes. If truth be told, her words stung a little. I kept my eyes closed until she walked to the door. I could feel the warmth of her and smell the orange blossom. Opening my eyes, I saw the ring still lying on the table. "Don't forget her ring."

"Selene wanted you to have it," said Bria, not a speck of emotion in her voice. She walked through the door, leaving me alone with my inner demons.

Time ticked by, all the while I remained standing against the wall with my eyes clamped on the lapis ring. Finally, when I could feel the sun rising, I barred the door before slipping into my sleeping bag. A dreamless sleep was not to be had. My mother visited me that day, bringing a long-dead memory with her.

"Do you know who this is, Caesarion?" Cleopatra asked. She was holding me in her lap as we sat at the foot of a statue Mother visited

frequently. The stone kept the room cool. In the heat of a summer day, it was my favorite place to be. I gazed up at the larger-than-life granite woman, the mother goddess nursing the god Horus. The statue was enormous, five times the size of Mother. I knew it was smooth to the touch because I often ran my hands along her cold leg. At the moment, I was more interested in playing with Mother's tightly braided, beaded hair, which fell around her shoulders.

"Our goddess Isis," I answered in my little boy voice.

Mother took my hand and pressed it to her lips. Torches lit the space around us, casting dancing shadows on the walls. Fresh lotus flowers surrounded the base of the statue, mingling with the scent of Cyprinum, poured into a milky white alabaster bowl. Cyprinum was one of Mother's favorite scents, comprised of cardamom, cinnamon, and myrrh, among other spicy fragrances.

"That's right. But, she's more than our goddess. She is me, and you are the son of both the goddess and the woman." She held me to her cheek, stroking my back with tender care. "Never forget who you are, Caesarion. Never forget who you are," she said as we rocked side to side.

But I had forgotten. I had forgotten and denied my origin, my parentage, my past. Once I was turned by Layla, I chose to throw my true self off like an old coat. My family was dead. I was believed to be, too. Egypt, the country I once held so dear, seemed a stranger to me. There was no going back.

Becoming Alexandre was easy, too easy. I slipped into a decadent laziness with an ease that was staggering. Was Millicent to blame? My love for her was a simple excuse. I blamed my lackadaisical ways on waiting, always waiting for Millicent to move on and toward me. Really it was more than that; a closing of the heart and mind, a distraction. Besides, I was shiftless long before the Marchioness came around.

There was a reason I never spoke of who I was; I felt Caesarion and all he represented died when I became Alexandre. I didn't want to think about it, didn't want to remember. There was only pain in remembrance, something

I never understood about Millicent. To hold on to a love that could no longer be made no sense to me. And yet, I had held on to her. It was time to change that.

With the sun again on the other side of the world, I left the crumbly stone cabin with only a small pack on my back. I should never have come here; the era of Millicent and Annie was over for me. It had been months since the episode at the plantation, and it was time to reinvent myself once more. Something new waited on the horizon.

I found Bria in a one-star motel on the outskirts of Paris. I cringed. Surely the woman could have found better accommodations. Knocking on the door, I had to cover my nose with the sleeve of my jacket to protect my senses from the urine smell coming from the gray, threadbare carpet. This was not the Paris I knew, nor would I normally be caught dead in a place like this.

After receiving no response to my knocking, I resorted to pounding. My top-of-the-line hiking boots found their current situation offensive, although I doubted the situation inside was much better.

Several minutes of banging later, a sweaty gentleman poked his bald head out of a door down the hall and yelled several obscenities in French.

Before I could lob my own response, Bria finally opened the door. I grunted, stared at her pointedly, and shouldered my way into the dingy boxlike room. I was right about the space within; the view was not much improved.

"Come right in, your highness," she said sarcastically.

I tossed my pack on the one crooked table, water rings and cigarette burns gracing the melamine top. It was more favorable than the floor, which I didn't trust the cleanliness of. Looking around, I sat carefully on the end of the bed. "I will, thanks." I responded with the same measure of sarcasm. "Was the Ritz all booked?"

The bed's orange coverlet was vintage about twenty years ago. There were yellowed stains on one of the walls and a box TV with rabbit ears, something I hadn't seen since the seventies. I doubted it worked.

"Not all of us are swimming in cash, stolen through the ages." She crossed her arms, leaning back against the door.

"I haven't stolen money in two hundred years, I'll have you know. When I did, it was called survival." I bounced a bit on the bed, coils springing underneath me.

"Change your mind?" She was dressed in tight black yoga pants with a form-fitting racerback top. Her red hair tumbled just past her shoulders in sexy waves. If there was one woman I didn't want to find attractive, it was this one.

I forced my stare to stay locked with hers, not allowing it to roam its way around her fit, toned body. "I wouldn't be here if I hadn't. When do we leave?" I paused. "It occurs to me I don't even know where we're going." I imagined the region where someone called the god of death ruled had to be hellish. Perhaps his abode was the skull-lined catacombs which lay under Paris or the inside of a sweltering, erupting volcano.

"We're going home," she said. "To Ireland."

I considered this for a moment. Ireland didn't fit with my idea of a hell-mouth type of location, with its verdant, rolling hills and fairytale castles. I couldn't recall ever having been to Ireland. I supposed at the end of the day I had that to look forward to. I could call it a vacation, sneak in some sightseeing along the way.

Bria continued, "Given your travel limitations, I thought we could take the train to London and stay the day. Then we'll leave again at sunset. I have a friend who will meet us in Holyhead with his boat. He'll take us precisely where we need to go."

I thought of my luxurious private plane, which was now in Millicent and Annie's possession. Air travel would've been a more practical way to transport ourselves to Ireland without all the stops and starts. My pretty stewardess, always eager to help me relax, was dearly missed. I felt annoyed for a moment, then got over it. Let them have it. I was beginning anew, after all. It wasn't like I couldn't replace it, if I so wished. I had piles of money, as Bria already pointed out.

As we had plenty of time to get to London before dawn, we left immediately to allow ourselves ample cushion. This suited me fine, as I couldn't exit the horrid motel fast enough.

At the station, Bria insisted on buying her own ticket. I longed to sit in first class but bit my tongue and followed suit, purchasing a seat in coach. The station was cold, but clean, and reminded me of every other train station I'd ever been to; the lighting was too bright, the seating uncomfortable, and no one smiled.

Once tickets were purchased and we were seated across from each other on the modern and comfortable train, I asked Bria if she wouldn't mind elaborating about this demon god I would soon be meeting. Best to know what sort of danger lurked. There were few people on the train in the middle of the night and no one in our immediate vicinity to hear us.

Bria pulled a book, old and worn, from her backpack and flipped through it until she found what she was looking for. "Here," she said. "This is Balor."

I took the book from her, peering down at the monster my sister had been trying to vanquish. Now, I'm no shrinking violet, but what I saw on the page made me want to recoil back into the seat until I became invisible. As if the title *god of death* wasn't frightening enough. "Is this an accurate likeness?"

"Yes, I drew it myself," she said proudly.

She should have been proud; the drawing was excellent. The picture of Balor was fully three-dimensional. This thing—he could not be called a man—was terrifying. Covered in pointed armor from head to toe, he sat on a throne of spikes. His horned helmet was barbed in three places. There were long metal thorns on the armor at his shoulders, on his one knee, and across the chest plate. The beast was a virtual porcupine of steel skewers. In his hand, he held a spear, and his one eye glowed like a hot, orange coal.

The most frightening part wasn't any of this. It was the glimpses of flesh seen through the seams of his armor—it was a viscous red, sinewy like muscle, not skin. He was, in a word, grotesque.

"I've never actually seen his eye from the front, only the side. He can kill you by staring at you. His gaze is a stream of fire. So, if you find yourself directly in front of him, move. Most of the time he wears the helmet down over his eye, so he doesn't kill off all his minions."

"He only has one leg," I observed, wondering how he was able to walk without help.

"Yes, but don't imagine it's a weakness. He moves just as well as you or I. Better even, faster." Bria leaned forward, her elbows on her knees.

"I've only read about beings like this in books, fiction books." Balor looked like a villain from a superhero film, adapted from a comic book. I imagined a man dressed like him, taking pictures with children at a theme park, rollercoasters rocketing by behind them. I was having a hard time accepting this as reality.

"I understand. Think about this. How would you explain yourself to someone who had never seen a vampire before?" she asked sincerely.

I understood her meaning. I, too, was a fictional being to many, but it didn't make it any easier for my mind to accept this. I guessed seeing would be believing. "You said something about a portal. This, Balor, is in another, what, dimension?"

"Precisely. We call the portal the veil. The veil is in Wexford County, Ireland. Right now, lesser demons are coming and going from the veil at will, running amuck in the country and spreading. Our goal is to seal the gateway with Balor on the other side where he belongs. Only those like you and Selene can see it, only those with the blood of a god."

I looked up at her over the top of the notebook. "You can't see it? This veil?"

"No, not the portal. But I can see the demons. Anyone can once they believe. Demons can still kill you, whether you see them or not. So, a lot of the village folk are attributing the strange deaths to anything and everything else. This portal re-opens every thousand years. There are other portals around the world. They all adhere to different rules, respond to different things. If ours isn't closed, who knows what will happen. I imagine his plans have something to do with the end of humanity, as most demony plans do. His goal seems to have expanded this time, and we don't know why," she explained, leaning toward me.

"Maybe he's bored," I reasoned. "I can relate to violence-induced boredom."

Bria leaned back, rolling her eyes and looking out the window. "I'm sure you can."

I closed the book, tossing it on the seat next to her. "No one's perfect." I grinned widely, although she wasn't paying me any mind. My smile died as I thought that maybe I belonged with Balor, in the demon dimension, unable to hurt any more human beings.

Bria nodded off while I flipped through her notebook. I wasn't eager to meet any of the beings depicted in the pages, although they didn't all look so bad. Some of the fay were even cute and the will-o-the-wisp was quite beautiful.

A couple of hours later, we were in London. This was a city I traveled to often. London smelled like pavement and rain, something I rather loved. The streets were busy with people and traffic, even in the middle of the night. I refused to stay in a fleabag and told the driver to take us to the Ritz. Bria looked over at me. Her pride would have to take a backseat.

"Don't worry. Two rooms, on me. Order all the room service you like." I flashed another smile, to which she raised an eyebrow. Gladly, there was no objection.

Having stayed here many times, the room was everything I expected. I slipped off my boots, the plush carpeting massaging my toes with every step. The cool softness of the bed was a luxury I wanted to revel in, considering what lay before us. Not for one moment would I think of the redhead with the sexy brogue next door. I had left Bria to herself, happy to black out for the day surrounded by taste and fine linens.

CHAPTER FOUR

Pounding on my hotel room door pulled me from a delicious dream of red hair and long tangled limbs. I shook my head to clear it. I refused to be attracted to the abrasive woman now kicking my door. It was true, I had pounded on hers the night before, but the locations were very different. Surely, she could show some tact.

"Open up, lover boy, time to get a move on!" she yelled from the hallway.

Annoyed, I stripped back the sheet and rushed to the door, not bothering to cover myself. "People in places like these don't appreciate screeching in the hallways."

Bria met my nakedness head on. She neither looked away nor blushed. "I don't screech. Let's go, we only have so many hours to make it to the coast. I'll be in the lobby." She turned on the heel of worn combat boots and stalked off. Those boots had left black marks on the bottom of the pristine white door.

Disgruntled, I pulled on jeans and a hoodie, draping a rain jacket over my arm. I took a moment to look in the bathroom mirror as I ran my fingers through my thick crop of yellow hair. What on earth was I doing here? I only half-believed this fantasy about demons. What had me more curious than anything was the possibility of seeing my sister. The disappointment would be keenly felt if this all turned out to be a sick woman's delusion.

Ten minutes later, I joined Bria downstairs. The finely decorated lobby was full of posh men and women, all wearing their best designer clothes and bespoke suits. Bria wasn't fazed in the least by her surroundings as she devoured a granola bar, crumbs falling to the marble floor. She was wildly out of place here and I kind of loved it. Her flaming hair was enough to draw attention. Her clothing, which screamed survivalist, made her that much more conspicuous.

I moved up behind her. "You deserve a spanking for the ruckus in the hallway."

"The man who spanks me is suicidal," she said in a loud voice, drawing even more looks from the guests and staff. Bria began walking toward the glittering revolving door, not bothering to see if I followed.

We took the train to the coast, making it just in time. Bria chided me the entire way for "sleeping in". I couldn't wait until we were on the boat with what I hoped was a roaring motor.

Holyhead was a large seaport along the coast of Wales. I would've enjoyed exploring the town, particularly its Roman history. Unfortunately, we weren't here for pleasure. In the back of a cab, I craned my neck, taking in as many of the delightfully historic buildings as I could on our way to the docks.

The harbor was deserted at this hour, eerily quiet except for the lapping water against the sides of the many vessels. Boats of every size sat snug in their slips, rocking side to side. I could taste the saltiness of the air on my lips and looked forward to this leg of our journey. It would be cold and wet, and we would be outside, but this was nothing for one such as me. I'd had enough of traveling by encapsulated rail car.

Bria's friend was waiting for us at the dock in the vessel

she called a boat. I guessed, technically, it was a boat. It did float, although I wasn't sure for how much longer.

It was so dingy, it was almost black with large swaths of peeling paint down the sides. I suspected at one time the primary color may have been white. I stepped inside, afraid my foot would break through the rotting wood of the deck. "What a lovely ship," I said under my breath to Bria once we were seated behind the captain and I had pulled on my jacket.

We were invited to sit inside, out of the weather which threatened rain, but the musty odor issuing from below reminded me too much of a mausoleum. If we were going to sink, I preferred to be on deck. No more tight spaces for me.

"At least it runs. That's what matters," she said in a quietly clipped voice.

I kept further comments to myself as I concentrated on looking out at the water. I hadn't had much time to think and I didn't want to do much reflecting. Unbidden thoughts of seeing Selene along with fighting some death demon crowded their way in. If this all proved to be real, that was.

I couldn't help but wonder about Selene's appearance. Would she look like Mother? The last time I saw her, she was a child of only a few years, being torn from our mother's arms by a servant. Tears streaked her soft brown cheeks, her mouth open in a scream. That was now over 2000 years ago. Mind boggling how we both survived so long. And the creature, Balor, was he really as frightening as Bria made him out? If so, he would certainly be the worst thing I have ever faced. Worse even than Annie's old foe, Emilia Romanov, who I had made a point to avoid. I wasn't the knight-in-shining-armor type. Even if this death god was hunting down the living, I wasn't sure I much cared.

Strange where life now brought me. All those comfortable evenings spent with Mills in our cozy home were long gone. I rubbed my eyes, hard. I did not want to think about her.

"What is it? You're not going to bail on me, are you?" Bria was pulling a down jacket over her shoulders, shaking with the cold.

I sighed, making a point to look back at the water. "I'm not going to bail. Thanks for the confidence, Red."

Without pause, she said, "Do not call me that."

I turned my head to look her in the eye. "Then don't call me lover boy."

She inclined her head. "Whatever you say."

"You know, you don't have to be quite so abrasive. I get you're tough. Everyone who sees you gets that." Every time I moved, the chair underneath me, bolted to the floor, groaned in a way which reminded me of a wounded animal. I was a large man; this stool didn't stand a chance.

She didn't so much as shift in her seat. "You know, you don't have to be such an ass. I get you're arrogant. Everyone who sees you gets that," she parroted back.

I pulled a face, narrowing my eyes. "I don't have to help you. Maybe it's best if we don't speak for the remainder of this luxury cruise."

"Perfect." She rose from her seat to stand beside the captain as he began to pull us out of the harbor.

I hadn't taken much notice of the man, but he was young and rather attractive, in a rough sort of way. His eyes lingered on Bria a little longer than they should have, not that I cared in the least. They spoke in hushed voices, not that it mattered, because I could hear their every word. The conversation was nothing other than boring chitchat. I smiled, crossing my arms smugly. If she was trying to make me jealous, she was failing.

The seas were choppy, and the ride was uncomfortable. If I were human, I would have been sick over the side at least a dozen times over the few hours it took us to cross. Bria's fortitude impressed me. She didn't seem fazed by the rocking even once.

When we docked in Wexford, I felt almost grateful for the dry land. Well, not dry, it was raining cats and dogs, but it was solid. During our goodbyes with the captain, Bria slipped him an envelope. His hand brushed hers during the exchange and I could swear she blushed. I shouldered my pack and then hopped out of the boat.

The air was fresh and briny. Waves crashed onto the shore, splashing up over the dock. I slipped and slid my way down the drenched boards, raindrops the size of golf balls assaulting my eye sockets.

"Does it always rain like this?" I asked grumpily over my shoulder.

Bria was doing her own slide-walk behind me. "Not always. Don't tell me you're afraid of a little rain? Will you melt like the Wicked Witch?"

I chose to grumble by way of an answer. This was not in any way enjoyable. It didn't seem likely to get much better.

The night was cold, and Bria shivered noticeably as we walked to her car.

I removed a pair of insulated gloves from my pocket. I may have nicked them from the boat, just to be an ass. "Here, put these on," I offered.

"I'm fine." She shoved her bare hands into the pockets of her thick, puffy coat.

"Suit yourself," I said, stuffing them back where they came from.

This woman was grating my nerves. I hoped my sister would be a little more my speed; pleasant and personable. I still wasn't quite convinced I would be meeting my actual sister tonight. I only believed in the fantastical to a point. My sister and this Balor were a point too far. Perhaps the person I was meeting believed she was Cleopatra Selene in a previous existence.

I remembered Annie telling me of a past lives quiz she had taken after Jack waltzed into our lives. Her quiz result told her she was once Joan of Arc. We had a laugh at this, although the quiz had nailed some of Annie's aspects. She was a woman whose skills were honed during a war for independence, and she was loyal, brave, smart. I wondered if the woman I was meeting tonight had deluded herself into believing some nonsense pulled from the Web. The ring could have been stolen from a museum or private collection.

We came to a stop in front of a vehicle that, if possible, looked worse than the vessel we'd just disembarked from. Any insignia had fallen or rusted off, so I couldn't tell what it was, only that it reminded me of a metal shoebox.

"Can we go back to the Ritz?" I complained, opening the rusted door, which gave a piteous groan of metal on metal.

"The older the fiddle, the sweeter the tune," Bria said, smiling at me for the first time since we met. "It's an Irish proverb," she explained.

My brow wrinkled. "If you call the tune of this"—I moved the door back and forth on its hinges as it creaked and cried—"sweet, I would hate to hear what you thought was awful."

She rolled her eyes, dropping into the driver's seat. "A kind word never broke anyone's mouth."

"Let me guess," I said, taking my own seat. "Another proverb. You seem happier since we left the boat, I guess that's a good thing." Her mood had gone from sour to almost peppy the moment we docked.

"I don't like being away. All I feel is anxiety in my stomach, like one big knot of puke. It's easing now." Bria started the car then flipped it into reverse.

"Lovely," I murmured, wanting to get the show on the road.

Thankfully, we drove the rest of the way in silence, well, verbal silence. The car sounded like death on wheels; wheezing, popping, and even backfiring twice, sending me almost through the roof in fright. It only took about thirty minutes before we were pulling up to a rather nice country house in the middle of nowhere.

From what I could tell in the dark, we were surrounded by low lands with a smattering of rolling hillside. The vegetation consisted of grass and hedgerows. All seemed fertile and verdant, which was in keeping with what I expected to see here. The oak and sycamore trees dotted around the house were solid with the kind of branches humans build playhouses in. The cottage itself was Georgian in style, the exterior a yellow stone with a gray sloping roof and a rounded red door. Dawn was threatening to approach, so I didn't hesitate to make my way up the front walk.

The door opened as we drew near. I sucked in my breath, sharply. In the light of the doorway, almost silhouetted, stood my... mother. I knew, of course, this woman was Selene, not Cleopatra, but the resemblance almost knocked the wind out of me. I stopped halfway down the flagstone path.

"My god," I whispered. She was clearly no imposter. This woman was Selene and my brain had trouble wrapping itself around this fact.

"Come inside, Caesarion." Her voice was liquid silk, her posture relaxed.

I flinched at the name from her lips.

"I'm sorry," she breathed. "Alexandre." She stood aside to let us pass. I walked into the front room, which was nothing like I expected. I suppose I expected to see Egypt, to see our past; framed bits of papyrus on the walls, floor pillows, oils in bowls, incense burning, but the room was typical country. The furnishings were muted in color, the sofa and chairs soft, overstuffed. Floral throws, a quilt rack full to bursting with patchwork blankets, and a braided rug completed the look. There was a vanilla scent hanging in the air, probably from a candle or potpourri, which fit the scene perfectly.

"Let me take those." A chill swept through me when she spoke. I wondered if I would ever become accustomed to hearing the voice of Cleopatra fall from her lips. The voice, the appearance, it was startling. Selene took my pack and the jacket I had removed and was carrying over my arm, hanging them from the shabby chic hall tree. She wore loose cotton pants with an oversized baby-blue sweater, comfortable and relaxed, like her furnishings.

"Please, Alexandre, sit down. We don't have much time before dawn. Would you like to talk now or tomorrow evening?" She stood in front of me, tall and lithe. Her dark-brown hair was cut close to her head in a modern style, and her warm, tan skin glowed in the soft light of the table lamps.

"I'd like to talk now." I had finally found my voice.

"I'll split, if you don't mind, Selene. I'm shattered," Bria chimed in, still standing by the door.

"Go sleep," said Selene. Bria bounded up the staircase, two at a time. "Brother, please sit," she said again.

Brother. Something inside me broke at that word. Without knowing what I was doing, I reached out, pulling Selene into my arms. She stiffened and then let herself melt into the embrace. I breathed her in, her scent nothing like our mother's, but all her own; driftwood and sea air.

I released her, stepping back. "You must know how you look like her?"

"I do," she said as we sat opposite each other. "Keep in mind how young I was when we were taken and how long it's been. But I do have a sort of fixed image in my mind of her, an image and a scent of exotic oils and spices. And you, brother. I never knew your father, but you look exactly like every image I've ever seen of Julius Caesar."

I looked away. "I suppose. I didn't really know him." Julius Caesar was the last person I wanted to talk about. I pulled the lapis ring from my pocket and passed it to her. "Please keep the ring. I have Mother's bracelet. You should have this."

She took the ring and slipped it onto her index finger. "You have the snake bracelet?"

I nodded. "Yes, it's in my pack." I moved to get up.

"You can show me later." She placed a hand on my arm. "Do you have anything of Caesar's?"

"No," I answered, simply.

"I've nothing of Antony's, either." She sat primly, her back straight, her ankles crossed.

Our eyes met for a moment, then I asked. "What became of you? You seem to know I was out in the world, but you never came to me. Why?"

Selene looked down, spinning the ring around her finger. "I really have no excuse for why I never sought you out. I don't know you, Alexandre. I knew you as a child, two millennia ago, and even then, I have no solid memories of you. Knowing we were both immortal, I suppose I felt like I had all the time in the world to go to you. Then time got away from me." She shrugged her shoulders.

I couldn't really blame her for never reaching out. Could I have said I would? I wasn't sure. It seemed we both wanted to put the past away.

Selene leaned to the side, settling her elbow on the arm of the sofa. "As to what became of me, you and I had the same maker."

"Layla?" I interrupted, shocked.

"Yes. That's a longer story. I'll start from the beginning and try to keep it brief." Selene pursed her lips together and then continued, "The boys and I were given to Octavian's sister. Watching children paraded in chains elicited sympathy from the people of Rome, so we were not kept in captivity. Unfortunately, for our brothers, that sympathy didn't extend very far or for very long. I suppose there was still a fear in Octavian that one of them could challenge his power. I woke one morning to learn the boys were gone. I was told they were sent to live elsewhere and would never see them again. Even as a child, I knew what that meant. I lived in fear I would be next. Each day, I woke with a terror in my heart, but it never happened, and no one ever came to drag me away. I did what I could to be pleasing and helpful.

"When I was seventeen, I was married to King Juba II. We lived in Mauritania where I was well loved and a good ruler. I have no complaints of that time. I was treated well. In my thirty-second year, I became ill. As I lay in fever, I was visited by a girl. She told me her name was Layla and asked if I would like to join her and my brother in immortality. In my haze of sickness, I agreed. She took me to her cave on Kovos to work the change. You were gone by then, but I remained with Layla until she grew so mad that she, well, she snapped." Selene paused her tale, allowing me room to comment.

"Yes, I heard. I also heard she killed her progeny who remained with her on the island." I sat forward, engulfed by her story.

"It's true. There were a few others at the time, and she killed them all. She would have killed me too, except I was away. I found them when I returned. Well, I found what remained, which was ash, bones, and teeth. She blocked off the entrance to the cave and started a conflagration." Selene looked sadly down at her lap.

"Yes, this was my understanding. It's a shame. Not only was Layla ancient, about as ancient as we are now, she was turned too young and the choice was not hers. The years had become unbearable for her. You were lucky to be away. I wonder why she sought you out. Did she say?"

"Oh, Layla was always speaking some sort of gibberish. Half of what she said made no sense, or only made sense to her, and when I asked where you had gone, she said she didn't know. I believe I was a sort of replacement. The children of Cleopatra; that meant something to her. Maybe that was enough to explain why she came to me."

I nodded. "Layla always called me her special one. You're right. There was really no rhyme or reason to anything she did."

"How did you hear about what happened on the island?" Selene asked.

I looked off into the distance. I could remember hearing the story in a bar on the coast of Kovos like it was yesterday. Yet, I hadn't thought about it for years. "I returned to the island about one hundred years later. I heard the story as a sort of local legend. Do you worry about such madness, Selene?"

"I do. Although I try not to dwell on it too much. I'm not sure if we can do anything to stop it."

I worried about it, too. I hoped being turned after we were fully formed would save us. I wasn't sure how old the Russian Romanov had been. If she was young like Layla, that would help strengthen my theory. Maybe it was only a matter of time for us all, no matter the circumstances of our change.

We were forced to pause our conversation as the sun was rising. Selene showed me to a small bedroom on the second floor. While it wasn't the Ritz, it was comforting and inviting. I was beginning to feel very glad to be here.

A.D. BRAZEAU

CHAPTER FIVE

The next evening found us picking up where we left off. Selene and I sat in the breakfast nook, moonlight streaming through the stained-glass window and throwing dancing specks of color around the room. The light reflected off the vintage milk glass mug Bria held in her hands as she stood over us.

"Didn't one of your progenies defeat Emilia Romanov?" Selene sat back against the bench, watching me with her keen brown eyes.

Her question brought Annie forth in my mind. I saw her with those auburn locks tumbling around strong, capable shoulders, a teasing smile playing on her heart-shaped lips. Annie was a smart, formidable woman. I wasn't terribly surprised to learn of her rescue of the Hessian soldier and her ultimate victory over his evil mistress. "Yes, my Annie. Although, she was never really mine."

Selene nodded her head, understanding in her eyes. "You know, or maybe you don't, Emilia was a contemporary of Layla's. They shared a maker, perhaps the very first of our kind."

The shock had to be visible on my face. I crossed my arms, placing my fingers over my lips. "You're kidding."

When Selene shook her head, I said, "So, you're saying, in a demented way, Emilia was our aunt?"

Selene's laugh burst forth with so much force, she shook the table. "I suppose you could say that. The story I heard from Layla goes like this—keep in mind Layla's madness, so who knows how much is true. According to her, they were born in Egypt during the Middle Kingdom, 2,000 years before us. She and Emilia were slaves of Mentuhotep II. He tried to prolong his mortal life by performing a blood ritual inside his tomb. He rather succeeded. He managed to raise a demon which took hold of his body and soul. There were a dozen slaves inside the tomb as this occurred. Pharaoh, now possessed by the demon, turned on those there to serve him. He drained them all, then went out into the night.

"Emilia and Layla, alive but just barely, dragged themselves to the altar and drank from the chalice containing Mentuhotep's blood. I asked her what made her think to do this. Her response was they were not thinking, only acting. From that night on, they were immortals. Layla found her cave and made a rudimentary home for herself and Emilia. Eventually, Emilia became bored, wreaking too much havoc on the people of the island. Layla banished her and never saw her again."

"So, she wasn't an actual Romanov. Emilia adopted them, in a way." I shook my head. The history of our kind was incredible. The more I learned of it, the more I wanted to do something to preserve it. "Layla sought the island on her own and wasn't sent there, as Meskhenet thought. That's quite the story, Selene."

"We're full of them, aren't we?"

I chuckled. "I suppose so. Maybe one day Annie will give me the chance to tell her all about this."

Selene's soft smile warmed the room. "I'm sure she will."

"I came across an immortal before I found Millicent who told me of Emilia. This man was the last remaining progeny of a vampire who tried to take over her territory in

Russia. She destroyed them all and was after the poor man, the final kill on her list. He begged me to help him, to shelter him. I didn't. I was too selfish, too much a loner. I'm ashamed of that now."

Selene pulled her eyebrows together and leaned forward. "You couldn't have done anything, Alexandre. Not on your own. She would have destroyed you, too. What purpose would that have served?"

I was eager to hear more about Selene's personal story, not about the peril we faced, but my sister went into business mode.

"As Bria told you, Balor, in Celtic mythology, is the god of death. Only, he isn't a myth, and he is very real." Selene held her head in a proud, regal way as she spoke, which reminded me of Cleopatra.

"So, he isn't the only god of death?" I thought of other people facing a demon threat and shuddered. Clearly, my head had been buried in the sand.

"No, there are others throughout the world. Comforting, isn't it?" she asked rhetorically.

Coffee percolated on the counter, drawing my eyes to the other side of the space. The adjacent kitchen was surprisingly modern with stainless steel appliances and marble countertops. My guess was the room had been updated in the last year. Bria remained standing next to us. I noticed she was shuffling from foot to foot as she sipped her coffee.

"He knows all he needs to, Selene. We don't have much time," she said, impatiently tapping a Claddagh ring she wore on her right-hand ring finger against the glass. I noticed the silver ring for the first time. It was worn with the point of the heart toward the fingers. I believed this meant she was single.

Selene looked at her, and in a soft voice, she said, "We have time, Bria. Alexandre needs to know what we will be facing. He will have to be prepared, as much as he can be." She turned her attention back to me. "Balor almost destroyed this country in ancient times. He was subdued, pushed back into his realm by Lugus, his grandson. Only a god or demigod can defeat him, push him back, and seal the portal. His goal this time seems to be not only the destruction of Ireland but the world."

"Why now?" I asked. I was having a hard time getting comfortable. The nook was small. My sister and I both had long legs, so I had no other option except to stick mine out to the side at an awkward angle.

"We're not sure. We haven't exactly had a conversation with him." She smiled. "He seems to be, however, testing his boundaries. He sent a small force of river demons across the water to England. Bria and I intercepted them, using her friend's boat. They were weakened as they were not in their natural surroundings and we defeated them with little trouble. It's only a matter of time before he figures out how to successfully deploy his army."

"That was brave." I had no doubt whose boat they used. It was courageous to attempt to battle demons from the less than sea-worthy contraption we crossed to Ireland in. Selene didn't take my meaning, but I could see Bria glare at me out of the corner of my eye. "Okay. And we're what, demigods or gods?"

"You and I are considered demigods, those who are partially divine."

I leaned back on the bench. Partially divine. I thought of what I knew of demigods; only Hercules and Achilles came to mind. Hercules was known for his immense strength and Achilles was a great warrior, invulnerable except for his heel. I couldn't remember having any special strength or skill before becoming immortal. My physical gifts came from vampiric blood, not from the blood of the gods.

I pointed this out. "I don't have powers outside of what other immortals have. In what way am I divine?"

"A good question. It seems our divinity is not so much what we can do physically, but what we can do internally." Selene was a patient teacher. She sat unwaveringly straight while I continued to squirm, trying to find a comfortable position.

I thought of losing my head and how I was able to reattach it so swiftly. I knew to surely kill an immortal, one had to destroy the brain, but did my bloodline have something to do with my regenerative powers? Maybe that made me special. If I had removed Millicent's head that night at the old plantation, would she have recovered so swiftly, or at all?

"What else do I need to know about him?"

"Balor is the king of the Fomori, or sea demons. Every culture has its own mythology. You'd be surprised what's real. This is what we are dealing with here. The Fomori are lesser beings he can control by keeping well-fed with the bodies of his victims. He can also control a broader range of lesser demons, but the Fomori are his first knights. The Fomorians take different forms. The Fomori giving us the most difficult time right now have made their home in the River Slaney. These are the river demons I just mentioned. They're killing livestock, in general, terrorizing the people of the countryside. They will be a good foe for you to cut your teeth on. They are fierce and deadly, but not as powerful as Balor. Bria has told you about his eye, of course. It is imperative you never forget it. Always be aware of the eye in battle."

"And what help will I be able to provide, exactly? If you haven't been able to defeat this death demon, what could I possibly do?" I was trying to take this seriously by asking clarifying questions. It remained difficult to accept that I would provide any value in accomplishing this task.

"We've discovered the existence of a weapon." Selene opened one of the moldy books littered across the table, flipped toward the end, and then pushed the book toward me. "This amulet, when wielded by two demigods who share a bloodline, will ensnare Balor while also rendering the pair immune to any supernatural force. It has been placed in the center of the Celtic symbol for unity and strength."

The body of the symbol was the shape of an hourglass. From the top of this feminine shape sprouted two ovals in opposite directions which then met up again at the base. Seahorse-shaped holes were cut from the center of the ovals, perfect for a hand to fit through. The bright green stone was laid into the center of this hourglass.

"And where is this amulet? I take it you don't have it?" Add this to the growing pile of trials. I was already weary.

"We're still looking. We suspect the River Slaney Fomori may be able to tell us."

I looked up at my sister, dazed. I'd been willing to give this adventure a go, but this was all too much. "This all feels very complicated. I'm not really a complicated sort of man," I drawled, turning my head to look out the window. This exercise seemed futile. Couldn't we launch a missile at this portal and be done with it?

Bria snorted derisively behind me. "I told you he would puss out. Doesn't want to break a fingernail, and besides, too many women to sleep with and strangle."

I winced. Selene slowly closed the book, pulling it back to her side of the table.

"How much do you know about me, exactly?" I leveled my gaze at Selene, preferring to imagine Bria wasn't there.

"Enough," Selene said. "When I realized I needed you, I opened my mind to begin searching. Maybe it's our connection, but you were not difficult to find. Not only do we share a maker, we share our mother's blood, along with the spirits of Isis and Osiris. I was able to not only find you but investigate your life. It hasn't been a very good one, has it, Alexandre?" Her voice had none of the venom which Bria's contained. She possessed the same ability our mother had; to make me feel worse by speaking kindly.

"No, I suppose it hasn't," I said, once again looking out the window. Shame made it difficult to keep eye contact.

"You can change all that, you know. You can rewrite your story." Selene reached across the table, placing a hand lightly on my arm.

"You sound like a motivational poster," I said. Was this how wayward high school students felt in the school counselor's office? However, the concept was intriguing. Could I go from lazy, selfish, and murderous to something else entirely? Something greater? Part of me longed to talk to Millicent, to hear her opinion. I shook my head. I had to get that woman out of my mind. It was hard after so many years of looking to her for every little thing.

"I know, but it's true, nonetheless. And yes, you do," said Selene softly.

I turned my head sharply. "Please don't read my thoughts," I snapped.

She bowed her head, retracted her hand, and began stacking books. I made sure to seal my mind up tight. Bria stalked off into the kitchen to refill her cup with more coffee. While there, she flipped through her phone. A moment later, alternative rock was softly playing in the background.

"How did you become involved in all this?" I asked, my momentary anger passing. I found Selene's demeanor to be comforting, reassuring. Our mother exuded the same calming presence. Sitting across from Selene, I began to think I could rewrite my story for the better.

"I've spent the centuries walking the earth and helping wherever I could. I've wanted to make my immortality count for something. About a year ago, I was in Brazil, fighting a Boitata, when I heard about what was happening here. I wanted to help if I could."

Normally, do-gooders just made me roll my eyes. There was too much fun to be had and humanity sucked, anyway. Or so I always told myself. Selene clearly didn't see the world through the same lenses I did. Listening to her was beginning to make me feel even more like a heel than I already did.

"I'm not even going to ask what a Boitata is. Are we going to fight your river demons tonight?"

"Not tonight. The moon will be at its fullest tomorrow.

That's when we strike those beasts. I'm going to put these away." She stood, balancing her books in her arms and left the kitchen.

Her idea was probably to leave me with my thoughts. Instead, Bria plopped herself down in Selene's freshly vacated seat. I tried not to audibly groan.

"Makes you feel pretty worthless, doesn't she?" She smiled, seeming amused with herself, and continued. "To love oneself is the beginning of a lifelong romance...or is it? Do you still love yourself above all others, or are you beginning to feel like shite?"

"Another Irish proverb?" I asked.

"Oscar Wilde," she answered, sipping her coffee.

I nodded my head. I should have gotten that one. "I guess the answer to your elegant question is I'm starting to feel like shite. Have any more whiskey?"

Bria laughed and raised an eyebrow, which I found saucily attractive. "Always."

She leaned forward to pull her flask out of the back pocket of her jeans and handed it to me. The move was fluid, sexy.

"Those pants are awfully snug. How on earth does this flask fit back there?" I tipped the liquid into my mouth.

"Don't you worry yourself about what fits where."

Her comment caught me off guard, causing me to nearly choke on the whiskey. Bria was a hard one to get a read on. She was like Mills in that way, joking one moment, serious as a heart attack the next. My first instinct was to dislike her, but she was making it harder all the time. I could only assume she was under great stress.

"How did you get involved in this, Bria? Obviously, you're Irish, but how did you come to know about demons and such?" I took another drink from the flask.

"My father was attacked by a lake-dwelling Fomori at Lady's Island Lake." She paused, looking into her cup. "It ripped him to shreds. We were out nature walking, something we enjoyed doing together. This was about three years ago. I somehow managed to scare off the beast by throwing rocks at it and screaming. It was small, as far as demons go, about the size of a German shepherd, but my pop was gone."

"I'm sorry." No wonder she was all in with the demon hunting. I felt sad for her, and I wasn't used to feeling emotions for other people.

She nodded, continuing. "It was horrible. I never knew my mother, so after that, I was alone. A few other folks around here had seen some of the Fomori, mostly stealing animals from their farms. We got together to fight them. There were five of us in the beginning. We lost one, Danny, to the river folk. Then, I lost the others to Balor. We thought we could take him ourselves, without knowing anything about him. Stupid. I barely managed to escape myself." She turned around on the bench, raising her t-shirt to bare her lower back. The skin was covered in mottled flesh. "He burned me with his eye, but I managed to run away. That's one thing I can do, run fast. I was packing up, getting ready to turn tail, move on, when Selene showed up. She was able to push him back, subdue him for the moment, but in order to seal him back on his side of the portal, she needed help."

I handed the flask back to her. Bria tipped the remainder of the contents into her mouth.

"And here I am," I said.

"And here you are. If Selene believes you are worthy of a second chance, that's good enough for me." She slipped the empty flask back into its pocket.

I still wasn't convinced the three of us could defeat the god of death, but I was damned if I would let these women down. It may have taken me a long time to get here, but here I was.

Bria began swaying from side to side. "I love this song. My options are limited, dance with me." She grabbed my hand, pulling me to my feet with her.

The whiskey was no doubt affecting her. I could smell it

on her breath, heady and sweet. I could also smell the citrus of her hair, which was suddenly up against the side of my face. Bria's head rested on my shoulder, her right hand in mine, her left looped behind my back. I slid my free hand around her waist, resting it on the small of her back. I tried to resist but found my face turning downward, into her hair. This woman who I initially found abrasive had softened. She allowed me to see another side of her. The old Alexandre would turn this moment to his advantage. But seduction, although on my mind, wouldn't be a factor. I would simply enjoy this moment for what it was.

CHAPTER SIX

When you see something completely incongruous with the world you know, it changes you in a moment. My beliefs about the world were already being challenged, but they were about to be shaken to the core. Bria came down the stairs wearing her usual vampire-slayer style of clothing; tight black pants, a black sweater, a maroon vest, and black Doc Marten boots. Her thigh-strapped knife made its reappearance, along with a katana strapped to her back. That was new.

My own outfit was similar, minus the vest and weapons. Selene appeared not long after, looking more like she was preparing to lounge on her yacht rather than fight demons in cream leggings and a long silky tunic. She, too, carried a katana.

"Am I supposed to fight these things with my bare hands?" I asked, palms in the air.

"Of course not, brother. What sort of weapons are you used to?" Selene asked with a straight face.

Used to? I was pretty sure the only weapon I had ever wielded was my fangs, so that was what I went with. "These," I said, pointing to my elongated canines.

Bria snorted, shaking her head as if I disappointed her.

"We haven't all had the pleasure of living next to a demon dimension," I said snidely.

"No, we haven't. Some of us have had to suffice living a posh, comfortable lifestyle with nary a problem in sight," she retorted, the almost sweet demeanor from last night long gone.

"All right, children," interrupted Selene. "Come with me, Alexandre. I'm sure we can find something you're comfortable with."

I followed Selene toward the back of the house, Bria hot on my heels. I noticed the framed photographs on the walls of the hallway. They were an eclectic set of beautifully composed nature shots. They also didn't go with the rest of the décor.

"These are great, Selene. Did you take these?" I noticed several jungle and beach scenes that could have been Brazil. I stopped to appreciate a picture of a black and white toucan gripping a mossy bough with blue webbed feet, its orange and yellow mouth opened in a squawk. The colors were arresting, alive.

Selene answered as she continued walking down the hallway. "I did. My pictures are one of the few items I move around with me. I take them everywhere I go."

"That's right, you haven't been here long. Are you renting the house?" There was a lot to process when I first arrived. I had taken it for granted that the house belonged to Selene, but now I wasn't sure. The shabby chic furnishings didn't fit with her style.

"I bought it. It came on the market right after I arrived, about eight months ago. I felt like it was fate. It's perfectly located, not to mention isolated. Figured I could use it as an investment property. The house came as is with all the furniture, making it easy to move right in. Bria had an apartment in town, where I was crashing, but it seemed more convenient to have her stay here during all this."

"Speaking of all this, you know he has zero combat training, Selene. Are you sure this is a good idea? Shouldn't you train him first, before handing him a deadly weapon?" Bria spoke up behind me. I felt like she was telling on me to the teacher.

Before I could craft a response, Selene said, "As you pointed out last night, Bria, there isn't time. Alexandre will know what to do when the moment is right. I'm sure he's been in a few scraps, and he is ancient and powerful, as I am. He'll be fine."

I turned around, raising an eyebrow at Bria, who remained silent. My tongue threatened to dart out at her, but I managed to stay classy and keep it in my mouth. At the end of the rose wall-papered hall, scattered with Selene's photo collection, we came to a stop in front of a closed door. Selene pushed it open, revealing a room quite out of keeping with the rest of the house. Where the entirety of the cottage was warm, cozy, and bathed in floral patterns, this room was cold and sterile, the walls lined with weapons of all kinds. Swords, knives, even guns of every shape and size were organized according to type. The air in this room was antiseptic and at least twenty degrees cooler than the rest of the house.

"Guns don't have much effect with these creatures. They're also loud and messy, so we don't use them much. You're better off with a knife or a sword. A knife will put you a little closer to the action than you want to be. So, I suggest…this one." Selene pulled something resembling Excalibur from its place on the far wall. "This would suit you."

The sword was a solid, shiny steel which glinted in the artificial light. The blade was polished so well, I could see my reflection. The pommel was simple with a single Celtic knot design. It was heavy, but not too heavy for me.

"This will be fine," I said as I moved it from hand to hand. I felt like a knight of the roundtable and imagined myself leaving on a quest to slay a dragon. This seemed a nobler pursuit than what would no doubt turn out to be slimy, muddy, ugly river demons. I had always loved the story of Camelot, so Selene was correct, the sword suited me fine.

"Knights lived by a more chivalrous code than you, so don't get any ideas about yourself," said Bria. I was beginning to wonder if the woman possessed psychic powers.

She couldn't read my thoughts, but she seemed quite adept at reading my face. Selene stifled a laugh with the back of her hand. "Okay, okay. Time to go. Can I trust you two to get along when the moment counts?" she asked.

"You can always count on me," said Bria, looking my way, raising her eyebrows.

"I'm not the one..." I trailed off, realizing my reply would sound rather childish. "Of course," I finished, ready to get on with our quest. I took the scabbard Selene handed to me and pulled the leather straps around my waist.

"And what has led you to believe the river Fomori know where the amulet is located?" I was having a difficult time securing the scabbard and needed to buy some time by asking a question so Bria wouldn't have another excuse to laugh at me.

"They won't know exactly where it is, but they should know a general location. The amulet was specifically hidden from Balor and his fiends, but Balor can scry. Or so my texts tell me. I can speculate certain things about him through my readings. He's no doubt seen the amulet and its immediate surroundings through whatever means he uses to scry. Because of the enchantments placed on the stone, he wouldn't be able to see more than that. Since the river Fomori are currently giving us the most trouble, they win as the first demons we question." Selene batted my hands away from the buckle, securing the sword herself.

"Can he see us when he scries?" If he could, I wondered what kept him from coming after us here.

"I was told long ago by an old mystic that demigods are protected by that sort of magic."

I could add all this to the list of information I could

barely follow.

According to Selene, there was a band of several river Fomori about ten miles from her home. Bria jumped onto her back for the ride and we were off. Apparently, this was their preferred mode of travel. With Selene's preternatural speed and strength, they were able to cover greater distances more quickly with Bria hitching a ride. We would spring our attack on them, taking them by surprise. Selene insisted we leave one alive to question regarding the whereabouts of the amulet. She had some thin rope tied around her waist to use on the demon.

It seemed strange to me, tying up another otherworldly being with nylon rope, but I guessed she knew better than I did. We took off, the women leading the way. I enjoyed the run through the countryside. The wet ground smelled both peaty and sweet, the occasional pasture blasting us with the pungent scent of animals. I didn't mind this as the velvety green of the landscape was beautiful. I let my mind go blank for the first time since Savannah. Selene was right about the full moon. It shone brightly overhead, lighting our way.

A moment later, something hit me with the force of a semi. Or had I hit it? About halfway to our destination, I found myself flying backward on my ass. One moment I was running forward at full speed, marveling at the countryside, the next I was flat on my back, dazed and confused. Bria's scream brought me back to reality. For a second, I wondered if I ran into one of the many ancient oak trees until Bria screamed again.

"What's happening?" I yelled, scrambling to my feet.

"Get down, Alexandre!" yelled Selene, who didn't sound at all like herself.

I did, just in time. Searing heat hit my shoulder as I dove. Rolling under some brush, I smelled burnt flesh and realized it was mine. "What the hell is happening?" I whisper-yelled, desperately looking around for Bria and Selene but not daring to stand up.

"It's Balor." Bria's voice reached me, and it sounded

pained. I raised my head to get a look, then remembered what they said about the eye. That must have been what singed my shoulder. Staying undercover, I tried to listen instead. I didn't hear anything other than leaves rustling in the light breeze. Filtering out the usual nighttime sounds, I heard him. I could hear him breathing. His breath went in and out with a swooshing sound that reminded me of a cow when it breathes through its nostrils. Wherever he was, he wasn't moving at all. He was lying in wait as much as we were, and he smelled like burnt barbeque.

Not seeing him was driving me crazy. I had to catch a glimpse, even if that glimpse was only a foot. I needed to see some part of this devil with my own eyes. Silently, I moved from my prone position into a crouch. Ever so slowly, I began to raise myself up in the smallest of increments. When my eyes cleared the bush I was sheltering behind, I focused in, scanning the surrounding area. A slight movement ahead of me, back up against a sycamore tree, alerted me to his presence. At first, all I could make out was a formless shadow, but the longer I stared, the more focused he became.

He was monstrous. Never before had I seen anything living that was so bulky, so tall. He must have been eight feet in height. His width was easily that of three football linebackers. As I crouched in my uncomfortable position, staring, the eye began to emerge. He raised the helmet only about a quarter of the way up for a peek. It was enough. Light poured out of the eye socket, hitting the ground in front of him with a sizzle. The face and body of Balor were now illuminated, and it was all I could do not to gasp like a child.

He was devilish, indeed. His ropey, sinewy body was visible through the seams of his armor, as Bria's drawings depicted. I could see the workings of his muscles and veins as if I were looking at a skinless human. It was revolting. I dared not move a muscle. Never in my life had I seen something like this, but I wasn't stupid enough to try to run.

The eye moved around the clearing for a few more moments before giving up and turning away. Balor must have assumed we had fled for the time being.

What Selene told me about his eyesight made sense now. Because of the raging fire in his eye, his sight was poor. He could see, but his vision was dimmed, blurry. The beast relied on his other senses, hearing, most of all. If we stayed hidden and silent, we were okay. I waited until I was sure he was gone, then moved off to look for Bria and Selene.

"Where are you two?" I whispered. Maybe they had run off.

"Here, hurry." It was Bria who spoke.

I found her kneeling over Selene, who appeared to be on her stomach. Bria moved aside, and I sucked in my breath. "Selene, my god."

I dropped next to my unconscious sister. Her back and right side from the top of her head to mid-thigh was burned down almost to the bone. No mortal would have survived this. The charred smell was sickening. The wound, cauterized by the heat of the blast, wasn't bleeding, so that was a good thing.

"She flung me off her, taking the full force of Balor's eye." There were tears in Bria's eyes.

"She'll be fine in a day or two." I took another look. "Okay, maybe three. Are you all right?" I asked Bria as I gingerly lifted Selene in my arms.

"I'm fine. Jammed my elbow, but nothing's broken. You're sure she'll be all right? She looks…"

I looked at Bria, whose face was practically green. "I'm sure. If I survived losing my head, she'll survive this."

"Your shoulder." Bria touched my arm.

"It's only superficial. I won't need anything special for it to heal."

She nodded, looking away, then walked over to where I was hiding to retrieve the sword which had come loose and fallen from my waist during the chaos.

I continued, "Let's get out of here. You lead the way.

Why was Balor here? Do you think he was waiting for us?"

She shook her head. "No. We took him by as much surprise as he took us. I've no idea what he was up to, but he was definitely taken aback. Probably checking on his underlings."

We were about five miles from the house. It was a long way for Bria to walk, bruised as she was, but I couldn't carry her and Selene, so we took our time. I knew Selene wouldn't be waking up this night. Bria possessed a surprising amount of stamina for a human. She was strong of body, and equally, it seemed, strong of spirit.

Once we arrived, I continued to hold Selene while Bria stripped back the blankets of her bed. She laid down soft towels over the bottom sheet. I placed Selene on top of these, face down. Blankets would not feel good tucked up against those open wounds, so we left her uncovered. Upon my insistence, Bria went to bed and I went to the freezer. Selene kept a supply of blood there, taken from hospitals and clinics for her own emergency needs. I pulled out a few bags and warmed them up. When they were ready, I held Selene and poured the blood in her mouth, bag after bag. She swallowed unconsciously, never waking up. After feeding her, I opened my wrist, carefully letting my immortal blood pour over her burns. Her body soaked up the moisture readily. I was proud to not have spilled a drop on her sheets, although the towels would no doubt be tossed out.

With that task out of the way, I sat in her room, determined to watch her until dawn. I felt a protective instinct take over as I observed my sister's wounds slowly begin to heal. Injuries of this degree would take longer than usual to knit themselves back together. Since we were divine, I hoped this meant she too would be a quick healer. This woman was my family, my flesh. An urge to protect her welled up within me. I never would have thought in a million years to be reunited with another of Cleopatra's children. This was a relationship I would kindle. I hoped once we had fulfilled our mission, she would want the same. We could become a team, fighting evil around the world.

Evil; I thought I'd known what the word meant, but not after tonight. I didn't really want to contemplate what I had seen. But how could I not? Demons were real, they existed. I was no longer the evilest being I knew. There were worse things out there and I would have to face them again. I wasn't sure I would be ready, I wasn't tonight, but I was sure I couldn't turn my back on this, or Selene.

A.D. BRAZEAU

CHAPTER SEVEN

Three nights passed before Selene regained consciousness. Her muscles and skin had knit themselves back together, but the derma was still mottled and scorched. Each night she lay in her deep sleep, I poured several bags of blood into her open mouth. I knew this would speed the healing process.

Bria kept to herself for the most part during this time. She hadn't slept much since this all began. She used the nights I spent nursing Selene to catch up on needed rest. I couldn't imagine what we could possibly have to say to each other, so this arrangement worked out fine.

Tonight, Selene sat at the breakfast table. She bent forward, her burnt arm propped up, her healthy arm massaging the gnarled flesh. "We've lost so much time," she mumbled. "Bria says the McDonnel's lost all their sheep last night and Mr. Kelly was attacked by something he thought was a wild animal but couldn't actually explain. It's a miracle he survived."

The sun set thirty minutes ago. Warmth permeated the kitchen, the smell of fresh coffee and leftover cinnamon buns hanging in the air. What I wouldn't give to settle in with a good book, my feet propped on a stool. There would be no lounging tonight.

The evenings were beginning to feel as if they had a weight to them. I felt it around my shoulders, like a mantle. Selene was right. We had lost time. While she was recovering, Balor had been out with his special friends on the loose. Bria, roaming about during the days, heard story after story of slaughter. More and more locals were losing their livestock and two humans had lost their lives; people were afraid. The consensus was a serial killer, or killers, was stalking the area. Something very unusual for these parts. The news media would surely pick up on this soon. We had to do something, and fast.

"Do you feel ready to try again?" I asked Selene. I sat across from my sister, genuine worry for people other than myself blooming inside me for the first time in centuries.

"With the river demons, yes. We have to find the amulet and getting them out of the way will be a bonus." She moved her arm underneath the cashmere shawl she wore draped over her shoulders. I didn't think it likely she was back to full strength but waiting any longer wasn't an option.

Bria was once again pacing next to us, a cup of steaming coffee in her hands. I noticed her fair skin, usually pink of undertone, was beginning to take on a sickly, yellow pallor, and her eyes were bloodshot. Maybe she hadn't been sleeping like I thought.

"When are you sleeping, Bria? I thought you'd been using this time to rest, but you don't look at all rested." I didn't want to sound critical, but we needed her at her best.

"I'll sleep when this is over. It's kind of hard to shut off my mind for rest with evil lurking around every corner," she said, her accented voice hoarse with exhaustion.

"Evil lurking, or not. You won't do us any good in this state," I pointed out.

"I'll be fine. Worry about yourself." She looked me in the eye, determination burning in hers.

I shook my head, waving my hand. Apparently, she was

back to hating me again. "Whatever you say."

"Let's get armed and ready. I suggest we take a different route to the river and travel more cautiously." Selene stood, looking as graceful as always. These women were tough, no doubt about it.

This time, we managed to make it to within half a mile of the river area with no problems. I couldn't have been more grateful. Running into Balor was not something I cared to do a second time.

Stopping, Selene stood still as Bria slipped off her back. I had offered Bria a ride. She declined with a quickness that would have hurt my feelings if I had any. Selene proved to be as strong and fast as always, easing any worry I had over her.

"You both know what to do. But, don't forget, we need one alive." Selene looked at Bria, who nodded, then at me. I did the same.

I was chomping at the bit to get at these things. The last three nights playing nursemaid as Selene slowly healed were maddening. There was no better cure for boredom than slaughter.

Bria showed me a sketch of the river demons from her book before our first attempted outing. Compared to Balor, this was going to be a piece of cake. The biggest challenge would be their ability to go transparent and their slick seal-like skin, which made holding onto them tricky. Still, without the stream of fire pouring out of their eyes, this seemed almost too easy. The creatures were beautiful in a spooky sort of a way. They were also carnivorous, as all the demons were, which meant we had to watch out for their razor-sharp teeth.

I broke off from Selene and Bria, heading a little farther upriver. A sprinkle of rain was falling. I began to wish my feet were webbed. Gills would be helpful, too, in all this wetness. The moisture wasn't enough to obstruct vision, but enough to make the ground damp and slick under my feet.

The air smelled of earth and fresh running water. The vegetation here was denser than by Selene's cottage. The trees were full of thick branches and leaves, and a moss-like groundcover felt springy underfoot. Although I couldn't see the water yet, I could hear it rushing its way over rocks downstream.

Once I was about ten yards away from the women, I made my way with silent concentration to the river. The rushing became louder and louder, the scent of fresh water more intense. As soon as I had the bank in sight, I heard it, an unearthly breathing.

Turning only my upper body, my eyes took in the incredible sight; a glistening horse's head, dripping with water, half-transparent in the moonlight, was just beginning to emerge from the river. The eyes shined like scarlet rubies, catching the light from the moon with a sparkle. This creature was alluring and frightening at the same time.

The nostrils were huge, snorting big wafts of air in great puffs, and the lips were pulled back in a feral smile, teeth jagged. The initial impression of beauty gave way to pure terror. This was not a pretty horse, begging to have its head scratched. This was a beast from hell. The demon pulled itself the rest of the way from the river with a whoosh of water descending around it. It seemed to grow three times larger once on the shore. I no longer thought this would be a piece of cake and felt the instinct to run. I remained in place, determined to do my part.

I had taken the rope from Selene, not wanting her to get too close to another deadly creature so soon after her grievous injury. I knew this would be my trophy. The sound of fighting downstream pulled my horse's attention away. His friends were now engaged in battle. As he moved to leap toward them, I whistled. His majestic head snapped my way.

"Here, horsey, horsey," I said, my voice low, menacing.

He held his head high, his gaze glowing and hot, as I pulled the rope from my waist. The beast lowered his dripping snout, eyes never leaving me for a second. For a moment, I thought I could mesmerize him like my human victims, but that power was useless here. As he pushed air in and out of his nostrils in short bursts, one hoof pawing at the ground, I knew he was readying to rush me like a bull. When he did, I was ready, jumping out of the way just in time.

I turned to face him once more, but he was too fast. Surprisingly quick-footed for such a large beast on wet ground. He plowed into me like a double-decker bus before I was prepared, knocking me onto my back, exactly as Balor had done. The demon reared up on his hind legs with every intention of trying to squash me with his front hooves. As he came down, I rolled away and sprang to my feet. I jumped onto his back, intending to hold on as you would a normal horse and throw the rope around his neck.

As soon as I contacted its flesh, I slid off, landing in a heap on a pile of sharp rocks. "Son of a bitch," I yelped as the stones cut into my back with a stinging burn. This thing was slick, all right. I imagined getting a hold of this jerk was going to be about as easy as holding onto a sea lion. Now I was mad.

The horse faced me again. This time my back, now bloody, was to the water. If it knocked me into the river, where it was strongest, it could likely finish me off. I planted my feet the best I could, and this time when it charged, I stood my ground. I held the rope in one hand, out to the side, loop already made. When the beast closed the distance, I charged as well. Just as we were near collision, I crooked my free arm around its neck, swooping up onto his back in an acrobatic move I was proud of. The Wild Bill Hickok of the undead.

He tried to pull a trick by going transparent. I may not have been able to see him, but I could feel him. He was already in my power.

The rope was slipped over his head, tightening around its neck. I pulled back, restraining myself a little, as I couldn't see how tight the loop was being closed. I didn't want to pop off his head and lose all my progress. I squeezed its sides tightly with my thighs, not about to slide off this time. The beast ground to a halt, shaking its head with fury and kicking its back legs up in the air in a failed attempt to buck me off.

Jumping down, I pushed him onto his side. Fighting against fierce kicks and wetness, I finally managed to hog tie the beast as it wailed piteously. He was losing his transparency now that he knew he was had. I ripped off the sleeve of my shirt, securing it around the foul, dripping mouth.

"It took you this long to fight one demon? We're in real trouble."

I looked away from my catch to see Bria skipping toward me. Apparently killing these things put a little pep in her step. "I wasn't trying to kill it, I was trying to catch it," I said grumpily. "I was injured in the process." I turned to show them my already healed back, realizing too late how stupid that was.

"Selene had half her body burned away and I don't remember her complaining once." Bria stood on the other side of the prone horse, hands clasped behind her back.

I opened my mouth to retort then clamped it shut. This woman was infuriating, but we had other things to do. "How is a horse supposed to tell us where the amulet is?" I asked, making a point to look at Selene, not Bria.

"They can speak when they want to," she answered.

I looked down into the demonic eyes as they looked into mine. "Of course, they can. There was a time when I thought nothing about the world could surprise me any longer. I was about as wrong as it gets." I ignored Bria's snort.

"All right, time to tell us what you know." Selene knelt next to the head of the demon. She pulled my torn shirt away from his snout. "We are seeking an amulet that will seal the portal. Where can we find it?"

For a moment, the demon continued staring at me. I was

about to tell them I knew horses couldn't talk, when its eyes rolled toward Selene and it said, "I've never heard of such an amulet."

Let me tell you, it was quite shocking to hear a horse speak. But even more shocking was that its voice was very human. Selene was talking to this thing the way I'd talk to someone on the street.

"I'll let you live if you tell me," she said softly.

The demon seemed to consider this a moment. "Very well. I have heard Balor refer to the lost stone. He believes the amulet to be in a cave along one of the southern coasts. He doesn't know anything more than that, as he cannot see the exact location. I can tell you no more."

"Thank you," said Selene.

A second later, Bria tossed Selene her sword. In one swift movement, Selene brought it down, severing the head of the demon sea horse. It disappeared in a puff of smoke.

"Well, look who isn't perfect after all," I said, a smile playing on my lips.

"She couldn't very well let it live, it's a demon. What are we going to do with it, be friends while it wantonly murders? Killing demons and killing people is not even remotely similar," said Bria, crossing her arms.

I shrugged my shoulders, doing my best not to laugh. "I wasn't complaining. Only pointing out we all have flaws."

I continued to smile as I held out my hand to my sister. She took it, springing to her feet.

"That disappearing act was like a magic trick, makes cleanup very convenient," I said to Selene.

Selene giggled, in spite of herself. "Oh, Alexandre. You can see the humor in everything, can't you? Since demons only have a partial foothold in our dimension, their bodies return to their own when they die."

"Humor makes life more fun. Now what? Are we off to find this cave?" I asked, stretching my arms over my head.

"Tomorrow night." Selene paused, cracking her neck. "There are many caves along the southern coasts of this country. We need to do more research and no doubt we can expect another challenge when we do find it."

I moaned. "Not more demons."

"More demons. They will be different, of course. But the more practice for you, the better. At least we cleaned up the river demons and this one's revelation gives us a good starting place."

"Fantastic," I muttered.

Were these trials my penance? Would I find absolution on the other side? I didn't think life worked that way, as I'd already mentioned. But, what did I know about life anymore? Penance or no, Bria certainly didn't seem to believe I deserved to be pardoned. No matter what she said, her initial attitude toward me kept coming back.

Selene hooked her arm through mine as we readied to go back home. "We wouldn't be able to do this without you, Alexandre. You're exactly the pair of hands we need." At least my sister believed in me.

CHAPTER EIGHT

"Your collection of books is impressive. What are they exactly and where did they all come from, Selene?" I sat next to my sister on the sofa. With her head almost always bent over a book, I felt I was more familiar with the top of her head than I was with her face.

"They're mystical texts. Some speak of demons—what they are, where to find them, how to kill them. Some speak of enchanted objects, like the one we're searching for. A couple are spell books, not much use to us, but a helpful tidbit or two can be gleaned from them." She leaned back, massaging her neck and rolling it in a circle. "They come from all over. This one, I acquired in Brazil." She picked up a rusty-colored, soft leather-bound book. The cover was worn through in some places, threads from the spine sticking out from both ends.

"How about these?" I picked up two books. One was a handwritten text with textured, papyrus-like pages. The symbol on the dark-blue, cloth cover was unfamiliar to me. The second, also handwritten, was without a cover. Its heavy pages were bound together with thick twine.

"South Africa and India. The book I'm currently perusing came from Northern Ireland and cost me a pretty penny. It looks newer than the others because it's been recently re-copied from an ancient text near to becoming dust." She handed me the book.

I flipped through a few pages. "Is this Gaelic?"

"It is. I can teach you if you'd like to help me research."

I readily agreed. Languages were easily learned by immortals. I long held a theory that the cerebrum of a vampire must be as affected by our powerful blood as our bodies. At the end of the hour, I was able to read enough to help Selene search for clues regarding the amulet.

After another sixty minutes of looking through books, I started to feel the desire for blood rising within me. It could be like that sometimes when one hadn't fed. All of a sudden, the thirst for it could overwhelm. "I need to feed." Selene and I now sat at the breakfast table, her ancient texts piled in between us. "I've put it off as long as I could. Any longer and I'll be feeding on Bria."

Bria was off somewhere, for which I was grateful. The scents of her candy-scented blood and citrus shampoo were beginning to drive me crazy with hunger of all kinds.

"Do that and I'll kill you." Selene was absorbed, not bothering to look up. I was sure from her tone she wasn't joking. With her face scrunched up, as she studied the open text, she said, "I prefer you not take any life with all that's going on around here, even if you find yourself an evildoer. There's enough talk in the village. Evildoers are rare in these parts, anyway. If you must gorge, go for something wild. No livestock, okay?"

"Sounds fine. Where would I find myself something large and wild?" I asked, unfamiliar with local wildlife. The conversation was unsavory, but sustenance had to be found somewhere.

"You won't find anything larger than a deer, and they're not plentiful. There's no lack of smaller animals. Things like foxes and badgers."

I wrinkled up my nose, making a face. "On second thought, I'll just find myself a few young ladies to drink from. Slaughtering a skulk of foxes seems in bad taste, even for me."

Selene murmured her assent. She could do with a better sense of humor. I knew the situation was dire, but a little levity never hurt anyone. I missed my playful banter with Annie and Mills. Mills may have been depressed most of the time, but she was always good for a quip.

It was past midnight when I found myself stalking the outside of the quaint village pub. The building retained its old-world charm, as did most of the buildings in the downtown section of the village. The only modern aspects to the atmosphere were the electric streetlamps, which cast eerie shadows on the cobblestone streets. I stayed to the dark alleyways, managing to secure myself four Irish beauties to partially feast on in the span of an hour.

The last woman stepped outside the establishment to talk on her cell phone. As she pressed "end", I slid my hand over her mouth, turning her youthful face toward mine. Her soft, rounded body attempted to jerk away, but I was too swift, meeting her eyes with my own. Leading her into the dank alley, I pulled her up in my arms. She had a sweaty, but sweet odor, no doubt from the close, warm pub where she had spent her evening.

I drank what I needed for nourishment, without any enjoyment. I had not enjoyed any of my blood donors this evening, something I usually did. Wielding my power over others never ceased to bore me, until now, it seemed. Like the famous movie comedy, I had lost my mojo. The question was how to get it back.

Not only did it no longer interest me to take blood, I was equally uninterested in finding and taking my pleasure. Hopefully, this nonsense would pass. I didn't think it necessary to lose myself completely.

When I arrived back at Selene's home, I walked through the rounded front door I associated with hobbits and elves to find Bria asleep on the sofa. This lady had something against admitting she needed sleep. I witnessed her nodding off from sheer exhaustion just about everywhere. Earlier, I swore she dozed off over the coffeepot, refusing to lie down after being startled awake by Selene.

I stood for a moment watching her. I dearly hated to admit that I liked this woman. I didn't know why, as she wasn't very nice to me. How could I blame her for that? More interestingly, she seemed to be a mix of both my preternatural children. Maybe this was what partially drew me to her. Like Annie, she was fierce, strong, and independent. Like Mills, she was delicately beautiful, loyal to her friends, and seemed to be longingly reaching for something out of her reach.

"Alexandre."

Selene's voice made me jump. "Sorry. Come in here, I've found something."

I trotted along, following her into the kitchen. She'd caught me staring at Bria. I wondered what she thought I was doing.

"What is it? The location of the amulet?" I leaned against the door frame, trying to look like I hadn't been caught with my hand in the cookie jar.

"Yes, and no. The exact location isn't given, only a vague reference to a cave and cliffs. It isn't any more information than we received from the river demon. We need to start exploring if we expect to get anywhere. There are cliffs nearby at the Carrigfoyle Quarry. It would take nothing for you and me to run over there right now to check them out. I'm feeling restless, tired of flipping through these cracked and torn pages." She sighed, tossing the text she was reading back onto the pile.

"Let's go then. We need to leave Bria. She won't be happy when she finds out, but she needs sleep." I was happy to work off some of the tension building inside me, and climbing cliffs seemed a good way to do that.

Selene looked up at me with eyes a little wider than normal. "Agreed." A smile seemed to be forming on her lips, but she shook it away.

In the sterile weapons room, Selene gave me a quick and dirty rundown of the equipment we would need for our adventure as she loaded two packs.

"We'll go with the essentials since we're not going far; climbing ropes, harness, sling, locking carabiner, anchor materials, tether, and gloves. Being preternatural, we won't need anything fancy," she said as she held each item up for me. I thought this seemed like a lot of equipment and wondered what the non-essentials were. I tried to follow her, but she spoke and moved with such rapidity that she lost me. I would figure it out as we went.

"Speaking of preternatural. Wouldn't it be easier to scale the cliffs sans ropes?"

Selene selected two pairs of gloves from a shelf. "It would, but we can't risk being seen by a mortal night fishing at the lake. Best to appear like everyone else who has to use climbing equipment."

I understood her logic. Still, it seemed a waste of time and energy. I thought about how my life had changed in such a short span and chuckled.

"What?" She stopped mid-lecture to catch me in her narrowed gaze.

"I was thinking how not long ago I was seated in my favorite room, in a city I knew like the back of my hand, reading a book. My only care… Well, you know all that." I waved my hand. "Now I'm in a room full of deadly weapons, getting ready to scale some cliffs with my long-lost sister as we search for a magical amulet we need to slay a demon."

"Not slay, send back to his dimension and seal a portal. But I see your point. When you string it all out like that, it sounds crazy. Would you rather go back to that room or be here?" She zipped our packs.

I blinked my eyes, unsure of how to answer. "Ask me again after more time has passed."

She nodded, tossing me my pack.

Selene and I made our way to the quarry in minutes. The

forest surrounding the cliff-lined lake was dense and lush. We walked through the brush, our feet crunching pine cones and needles. The freshness of the air was a treat in this country.

I wasn't quite prepared for so beautiful a scene at lakeside. Even in the dark, I could see the blueness of the still water. We weren't here for recreation, however, and only stopped to gaze in wonderment for a moment before moving on. Selene said the cave we wanted would likely be shielded by magic. We wouldn't be able to see through the spell until the entrance was breached. Meaning there was no easy way to find the cave opening.

We set up to begin our first pass with the tallest cliff.

"There aren't any lake demons here for us to worry about?" I nervously glanced around.

"Not here that I've heard of. We should still be on our guard, just in case." Selene anchored our climbing ropes to the base of a thick tree trunk. She rappelled on one side of our first cliff and I rappelled on the other. Up, down, and across we went until we had scoured every inch of cliff face in the quarry. The work was tedious and time-consuming.

Human hands would not have survived. I had eschewed her offer of gloves, as I hadn't thought them necessary. As I searched, blood continually oozed from cuts and scrapes, simultaneously healing and being scraped all over again. The stone was smooth in some places, jagged in others. Thirty minutes before dawn, we dropped at the top of our last cliff.

"And you're positive the text wasn't referring to a normal cave, one that everyone can see? Maybe we should check them to be thorough." I lay on my back, gazing up at the clear night sky. I made out Orion and Cassiopeia before Selene answered.

"I'm not positive. However, it doesn't make sense to hide such a powerful object where anyone could find it. Does it?" Selene had her back to me, winding up a rope as she sat.

I thought my sister sounded a tad snappish, so I dropped

it. "You would know better than I would," I conceded.

Five minutes later and we were striding up Selene's walk toward her cottage home. Spongy green moss grew in between the flagstones, adding to the fairy-tale quality. This was the first night without rain I experienced in Wexford. It was nice to feel dry.

Bria opened the door. "Good almost morning. Where have you two been?" Sleep had done her a world of good. Her eyes were clear and she almost smiled.

"Searching for the amulet. I found more vague information, leading us toward more vague locations." Selene walked past Bria into the living room.

Bria must have missed the annoyance in Selene's voice because she clapped her hands together. "Did you find it?"

Selene shook her head. "No luck. I'll keep researching after the sun sets."

Bria offered to take our packs so we could head to bed. I handed her mine but followed her to the weapons room anyway. I wasn't ready to sleep, feeling restless after our climb.

"I said I got this," she said over her shoulder.

"I'm not tired yet," I said like a grumpy toddler.

"Selene must have been pretty disappointed," Bria pointed out as she unloaded one of the packs. "She's been researching that amulet for a while. This may be the longest anything has eluded her. I'm sure she's chomping at the bit as much as I am."

"We all are," I said, taking a pack and pulling out nylon ropes.

"I'm sure you're ready to get out of here and back to your life. The lack of willing female company must be slowly killing you," she said with sarcasm in her voice.

Her comment stung me, not for the first time. "I could easily find some company in the village. I haven't been interested."

Bria looked at me for a moment, said nothing, and went back to her work.

"What about you?" I ventured. "Any love interests in your life?"

"No," she answered shortly. "This is my life for now. Isn't it grand?" She indicated the walls of the room like a game show hostess.

"I'm sure there has been someone," I prodded, hating to admit to myself how badly I wanted to know.

"There hasn't been anyone for a long time and I don't want to discuss my love life, or lack thereof with you. Not all of us hop from one bed to the next." She took the rope from me, placing it on a shelf with other ropes of all kinds.

"People change."

"Not so fundamentally. I doubt long-term monogamy is in your wheelhouse." Bria turned back toward me, meeting my eyes.

"Maybe I'll surprise you one day, Bria." I left the unfinished pack on the table, moving toward the door.

"I doubt it." I heard her say under her breath as I left the room.

CHAPTER NINE

"Bria take Alexandre out tonight. Head to the pub. I'd love for you to get some sleep, but I know that won't happen." Selene had piled her bunch of go-to ancient-looking books on the breakfast table, her favorite place to sit. "I have a lot of research to do. I can accomplish more if the house is still."

"I can't possibly go out for a drink when there is so much going on. Besides, we can help you research the cave's location." Bria sat across from Selene, doing her best to look busy by grabbing a book and sticking her nose in it.

"Alexandre needs a night of relaxation. I can see him getting antsy. Please, Bria, I need time alone." Selene massaged her temples with closed eyes. My sister was an introvert. All the action, all the talking, was taking a toll on her energy and patience.

All this took place while I stood in the doorway as if I wasn't even there. I didn't bother to contradict Selene. She was right. Antsy was a great descriptor for how I was feeling. A night out sounded like heaven. However, Bria wasn't my ideal companion. I would have much rather gone alone. Perhaps I would re-connect with one of the Irish lasses I had previously feasted on.

Bria looked over at me from her place across from Selene. She seemed even less pleased than I was. "Fine," she assented. "Just for an hour or two."

"Wonderful. Loosen up, let yourself have some fun," Selene said, leaning across the table to squeeze Bria's hand.

Bria drove us to the nearest town where she led me to a pub called The White Horse. The name reminded me, unpleasantly, of my encounter with the river demon. I didn't think I would ever look at a horse the same way, let alone ride one.

The pub was a low, brick building on the far end of the main street. It was here I partook of my meals the night before. I expected clientele to be lacking on a Sunday night, but it was packed to the rafters with people. Following Bria, we walked sideways through the crowd of bodies, cigarette and pipe smoke obliterating all other smells. We managed to secure the last two seats at the bar.

Bria plopped herself on the stool, heedless to the jiggling of her small but pert bosom and to the looks of the surrounding gentlemen. I supposed if you took away the apocalypse garb and imagined her in something else, she would be quite pretty. Her hair, flowing and thick, was her crowning masterpiece and her eyes, clear, but haunted, spoke of an interesting life.

I slid onto the stool next to her, leaning forward for the bartender's attention. I wasn't expecting the beauty who turned to face me. Dark eyes, a luscious body, blonde hair pulled into a sexy, messy ponytail. She reminded me of Mills, and I couldn't help but grin.

"What can I get you...handsome?" She added the *handsome* at the end, like she hadn't quite meant to say it.

"I'll take a pint of your favorite." I flirted, my eyes not leaving hers. I was rewarded with a bright smile and a bite of the lower lip.

"Oh, brother." I heard Bria groan next to me.

She moved off the stool. From the mirror, I saw her take a seat at a newly vacated table. That was fine with me. Her absence gave me more freedom to converse with the lovely woman now pouring me a beer. The bartender turned away, bending over, a little farther than necessary, to toss the bottle into a bin. I could use some good, old-fashioned fun. Maybe this lady could help me restart my motor. The last woman I'd been with was Kathryn. At that thought, I clamped my eyes shut, rubbing them hard with balled-up fists. Something fluttered, spiked with pain in my chest. I saw light dimming in a set of bright green eyes.

"Something wrong?" She set my pint down in front of me, a look of sweet concern on her face.

"No, nothing. Thanks." I pulled several bills from my pocket, laying them on the table.

Not wanting to meet those dark eyes again, I pushed myself up, gaze trained on the ground, and walked over to Bria's table. "May I join you, please?"

She looked away but nodded. I noticed she was still without a drink and pushed mine over to her. "Here, I haven't touched it. Truth be told, I don't really want it."

"Strike out with the bartender?" she asked, still refusing to look my way.

"I don't know. Didn't try," I mumbled, oddly ashamed of myself. Shame was not a feeling I was used to. It was rude to flirt with another woman in front of Bria. My actions made her feel awkward. I wanted to apologize, but I didn't know how to go about it. Instead of trying, I decided to leave it. Kathryn Hart was haunting me. I didn't know how I would ever be able to erase what I did to her from my thoughts, or what I could possibly do to make amends.

I normally behaved in any manner I wished with women, never having once met with a protest. Something had changed. It started with Kathryn, with killing her. Maybe it started long before her with Millicent. Wanting her so maddeningly, never being wanted in return. I used women because I could. It was easy and made me feel better, if only for a moment. Now the thought of doing that made me sick. Mills and Annie would never believe this. Not that they would ever hear it from my lips.

The silence at our table became unbearable. I crossed my arms on the table, grabbing hold of my elbows, grimacing. "I don't think this is what Selene had in mind," I grumbled. "Maybe we should get back and help her. Anything would be more productive than this."

Bria sighed, finally looking in my direction. "I know Selene better than you do. If she says she needs alone time, then she needs alone time. We'll give her another hour to look through her books, then go back."

I frowned, leaning back on the hard bench. I understood Selene better than Bria realized. She took a long drink of the ale. Setting the glass down, she spun it around in her hands. "I have very mixed feelings about you," she said, staring at the pint glass. This was probably the most honest thing anyone had ever said to me.

"You and everyone else." I smiled a wan half-smile, hoping to break the tension a bit.

She continued gazing at the glass. "You really killed that movie star, didn't you?"

I shifted in my seat, suddenly even more uncomfortable than I'd been. My jeans seemed to become increasingly snugger, cutting off my circulation. "Yeah." My voice was almost a whisper.

"Why?" She looked at me then, hazel green eyes boring a hole straight through mine. "She couldn't have been evil."

"She wasn't. I don't have an explanation, if that's what you're looking for, Bria. I'm not a good person, vampire, or whatever. I've done terrible things." I tried to look away, to focus on the crowd.

"But you're helping us now. Is it because of Selene?" Her voice was clear and bright over the din of the pub.

"Yes, it was, at first," I conceded, wanting to be truthful with her. "I was curious about her. I wanted to see her, talk to her. But, now..." I stopped, unable to finish my thought.

"But, now?" Bria prompted.

I raked my hands through my hair, taking a deep breath.

I turned my attention back to my companion. "Now, I don't feel like the person I was in Savannah." It was true. I hadn't felt like Alexandre since my head was liberated from my body.

"How? Why the change?" Bria made herself comfortable, propping her elbow on the table and sinking her chin into her hand as she waited for me to bare my soul.

"It's complicated," I answered. I wanted to be more precise, but it was hard to put everything I felt and everything that had happened into words. 'It's complicated' was my go-to explanation for almost every question posed to me by Mills and Annie. Bria wasn't having it.

"So, uncomplicate it. I want to know. Help me understand." Her eyes seemed to have changed. Were they softer?

Maybe putting my experiences into words would help me somehow. Therapists made a decent living for a reason. "All right, I'll try." I pulled the beer from her grasp and took a swig. "As you know, my beginning was a rather dramatic one, given my parentage and what eventually happened to them. Once I left hiding, and after I was changed, I floundered for a long time. I fell easily into decadence, living for myself and no one else. It's hard to explain what time does to you as an immortal. I think I got lost in time, and before I knew it, hundreds of years had passed.

"One evening in the mid-1700s, my heart was claimed with one glance. A young woman, beautiful, kind, unhappy, danced into my life in a rustle of silks and glittering jewels. I decided I would save her from her bleak marriage, when the time was right, as I had observed needed to be done. I would become her hero, whisk her away from her dreaded existence, and make her my queen. We would live happily ever after, in love for an eternity. Only, I waited too long. She met a man and fell in love, becoming pregnant in the process. Everything had gone wrong in the blink of an eye. Her husband discovered the affair, hurt her badly enough that she lost the baby, and imprisoned her lover. This, I thought, was my moment. She came to me for help and I was going to be the hero, after all. I killed the husband, his stupid friends, and then, I killed the lover. This was my mistake. I thought once I had her and she was immortal, she would forget him. She never did. I underestimated her depth of feeling for him. She longed for that man for two centuries, until she came across him, once again."

"She came across him?" Bria interrupted, scrunching up her face.

"Reincarnation. Same face, same soul, different personality, mostly. She fell in love with him all over again. So...I went a little crazier than usual. I killed Kathryn in a rage, then almost killed her, the woman I claimed to love. It was lucky that her boyfriend was able to cut off my head. But, anyway, there it is. I lost myself with Millicent. Maybe I had lost myself long before her, but being here, it's giving me a new sense of purpose."

"To be the hero," Bria pointed out, a somewhat mocking smile on her lips.

I rolled my eyes. "Maybe. What's wrong with wanting to be a hero?"

Bria shrugged. "Nothing, I guess. Heroes don't usually set out to be heroic, they just are. The work praises the man, so say the Irish."

"Whatever, I'm putting in the work. I want to help my sister and possibly even you." I leaned back, turning my attention to the packed room. It was easier to look at strangers than it was to look at Bria. The bar was hazy from pipe and cigarette smoke, the crowd boisterous.

Bria drained the rest of the pint in one loud gulp. "You'll never be able to erase what you've done, Alexandre. Life doesn't work that way. I think you're the one who said that. I'm glad you want to help us and all, but it won't wipe away your actions."

"I know. I'll have to live with the things I've done. But I want to be better." I flagged down a waiter. "Two more please." He nodded, taking the empty glass from the table.

Bria leaned forward, elbows on the table. "You were Pharaoh for a while, weren't you?"

"I was. For a short time, I co-ruled with my mother. It was a name only thing as she did all the ruling. She was grooming me, teaching me the game. I was technically Pharaoh after her death, but the young man who was impersonating me was murdered not long after returning to Alexandria. I knew the life of a prince, more than the life of a ruler. It's hard to keep all the events straight. I wasn't there for most of what happened. I was in hiding and there are different accounts of what occurred after Mother died."

"It's amazing, incredible to think you and Selene lived during such a rich period, that your mother was *The* Cleopatra. It boggles my mind. What was it like? Ancient Egypt?" She gazed at me dreamily.

"It was everything you've imagined, everything you've heard. We were a people ahead of our time in many respects. In the palace, we lived in luxury, everything we could possibly desire at our fingertips. My mother was very learned, and I spent a great deal of time with her and her generals, advisors, and books. She spent a lot of time in the Library of Alexandria. It was a great loss for her when it was burned. She was devastated. It was one of the only times I ever saw her emotional." I was relaxing, slouching a bit as I became more comfortable.

"You should write a book about all this. I told Selene the same, but she didn't take me seriously. She was younger when she left Egypt, so she doesn't remember as much as you. Her memories of Rome are clearer." Bria took a drink of her ale.

I shrugged but was intrigued by the thought. "Well, that's an idea. Maybe when all this is finished. I do like a good book. What I'm really looking forward to right now is the new season of *Doctor Who*."

"I love *Doctor Who*. Who's your favorite?"

It seemed I had found Bria's sweet spot.

Bria and I spent the remainder of the hour bantering

over who was the best Doctor. My favorite was the tenth Doctor, but Bria favored the fourth. We fell into an easy conversation. For the first time since we met, I felt I was catching a glimpse of a relaxed, almost fun Bria. I was genuinely sorry when the hour came to an end.

"Ready?" she asked, looking at her plastic, sporty watch.

"Sure." I would have liked to have stayed, but I was curious to find out what Selene had discovered. I supposed sitting here, drinking, was a waste of time with all that was taking place.

When we pulled up to the front of the little house, we could see the top of Selene's head bent over a notebook through the living room window. She must have needed a change of venue. Bright, artificial light from the room poured onto the front lawn like a spotlight. Selene appeared to be writing furiously. This could be a good sign.

Bria bounced up the stoop, pushing open the door with too much force, slamming it against the wall with a bang.

"Sorry!" she yelled to no one in particular.

"What did you find out?" I asked, coming in behind Bria.

Selene looked up, her eyes glistening with excitement. "I think we have a location."

CHAPTER TEN

It seemed Selene had finally cracked the code. No doubt she was pleased. This was a key piece of information, one which had taken her longer than she would've liked to figure out. She smiled at us over her books.

"Where is it?" asked Bria breathlessly. The suspense seemed to be killing her.

Before waiting for Selene to answer, she rushed into the kitchen and set the coffee pot to turn on at sunset. Selene and I followed. We knew Bria would need her fuel, and we knew exactly what she was doing. The kitchen hadn't been tidied in a while; dishes were piled in the sink, while bread crumbs littered the counter. Bria pushed the debris out of her way.

"I believe the cave is located at the Cliffs of Moher. According to this text, the caves we seek can be found on the side of an immense cliff face off the southwestern coast of 'the green isle'. I had to search through thirty-some books to find the reference."

"How far are the Cliffs of Moher from here?" I asked, leaning against the kitchen island, the crunch of coffee grounds being scooped from a bag behind me. I was excited to see this area. My only wish was that I could visit as a tourist and not an adventurer and demon slayer.

"About four hours by car," answered Bria, pulling an insulated travel mug from the cupboard.

"We won't bother with a car, however," said Selene. "It won't take us long at all to go by foot, as long as we keep out of sight."

"I'll carry Bria this time." I realized I may have said this a little too quickly. "Since you're still recovering, and the trip is longer," I added.

Selene was long past recovering, but she didn't say anything. Instead, she looked at me out of the corner of her eye.

"We'll leave as soon as the sun is down. I'll go pack supplies," I said as I hastily retreated from the kitchen and Selene's side eye.

I was glad to have had Selene's climbing lesson. I packed all the items we used previously, making sure I pulled enough tools from the shelves to fill three packs this time. By the time dawn rolled around, I had everything we would need neatly organized into perfect bundles. I would wear mine on my front, so Bria could piggyback to the Cliffs. Unless she wanted to ride in front of me, which I doubted. Standing back, I surveyed my work, feeling proud.

Making my way to my room, I was glad to see Bria passed out on the couch. I knew how badly she needed the rest. I stopped long enough to cover her with a patchwork quilt before retiring to my own slumber.

As soon as the sun set, we were readying to take off.

"Good job with the supplies, Alexandre." Selene couldn't help but check my work, digging through her pack, her soft silky tunic billowing as her arms moved. I grinned as she nodded approvingly.

"Looks like he's learning a thing or two." Bria stood in the hallway outside the weapons room, clad in her usual all black.

"Ye of little faith." I good-naturedly tossed Bria her bag.

Outside, she hopped onto my back without protest, which surprised me. Selene was right about the distance, and we were at the Cliffs in no time. The misty sea air was bracing, the sound of the water crashing into the cliff face below us drowning out most other sounds. Bria stifled a shiver, her lean arms hugging her chest.

The cliffs were impressive with immense, towering faces of shale and sandstone. I imagined the daytime views were likely stunning. This was one of those rare moments I regretted not being able to take in the sights by day.

Selene took a compass from her pocket, following the needle North along a ridge for about fifty paces. Bria and I followed my sister, who believed she had deciphered coordinates from the same text where she found the reference to our location. Selene came to a stop, closing the compass with a snap. "Based on the description given, this area seems the most likely. Maybe we'll get lucky."

"You had to jinx us, didn't you?" My partners ignored my remark as we all dropped our gear and began preparing for the ascent. The light from the stars and half-moon reflected off the water, providing my sister and me with all the light we required. Bria pulled out her small tactical flashlight, popping it into her mouth to illuminate her task.

I was able to strap myself into my own harness this time. I noticed there wasn't another soul anywhere near us. This was a tourist location, and tourists didn't visit natural attractions in the dark. But Selene was insistent she and I use the equipment for appearances, anyway. Scaling these cliffs was illegal, so we rushed through our preparations.

Coming down the cliff face was a fun experience, in no way diminished by this being my second time. This was something I would have to do again for pleasure. I wore gloves this time, as I had learned my lesson previously. Trusting an anchor and a boulder to hold my weight gave me pause at first. But as soon as I allowed myself to trust it, I felt a freedom I only ever felt while running and leaping through the air.

I looked over at Bria. Keeping up with me was no problem for her. Her face was flushed with the exercise, her brow furrowed in concentration. I was struck with concern. If I was to fall to the jagged rocks, sixty-five feet below us, my broken body would eventually repair itself. As long as I kept my brain from being smashed to a pulp, I would be fine. If she were to fall, she would immediately cease to exist. What felt like a pit formed in my stomach at the thought.

Carefully and purposefully, I turned my concentration back to what I was doing. I didn't want to have such concern for Bria. We were going to find ourselves in much scarier places than this. I couldn't allow myself to be distracted by such feelings.

"Here!" Selene shouted from the other side of Bria.

We made our way to where Selene had disappeared into the rock face. The cave opening shimmered like a trick of the light, a mirage brought on by extreme dehydration. Anyone looking from above or below would never notice it. I pierced the mirage with my hand. It felt like nothing but air. Bria went in first. I followed, wondering if we had triggered a warning by piercing this magical illusion.

"Guess I didn't jinx us after all," Selene said as she waited for us to unharness.

I grinned, hoping this meant she was loosening up a bit. "Don't get too cocky, we still have to find it." I paused, considering something. "Would anyone be able to move through this?"

Bria was stepping out of her harness. "Yes, but scaling these cliffs isn't allowed. It would be extremely unlikely anyone who wasn't looking for the amulet would find it. Besides, when it was placed here a thousand years ago, people didn't rock climb for fun." She had a point.

The mouth of the cave was smooth. Moisture seeped from every pore, creating a slick surface. There was a sharp, tinny smell which made me think of wet metal. After we unhooked ourselves, we took out flashlights. Selene and I didn't need them to see, but we did need to keep an eye out for spooks.

"Any idea where we're going to find this object?" I asked, pointing the beam of light toward the empty black space in front of us. I couldn't see far, but from where I stood, the hollow in the center of the cave looked infinite.

"None. All the text says is the amulet is in a cave somewhere in this area. We may not even have the right one. Who knows how many magically hidden hollows are out there?"

I threw Selene a look. "Seriously?"

"No, not seriously. Keep your eyes open. Let's go." Selene walked pensively ahead of us.

We drifted onward, streams of light dancing off glimmering wet stone. Water trickled with the sound of a soft waterfall. The cave, which started out rather wide, became close in a hurry. I felt a tightness pinch in my chest. A light-headed swoon swept through my head, causing me to stumble. I stopped, pressing my hand into the cold, dripping stone, grateful for the coolness.

"Alexandre, what's wrong?" Selene asked, shining her beam of light away from my face, but close enough that she could scrutinize any expression I may make.

"If he were human, I would say he was having a panic attack," said Bria from the darkness. "He seems about to faint."

"I'm not panicking. That would be ridiculous. I don't care for close spaces. It's not even possible for me to feel lightheadedness. This is stupid." I did feel stupid, but something about the closeness of this rocky tunnel had worked its way under my skin. I didn't like it.

"It's all in your head," said Bria gently. "I used to be claustrophobic, too. You must take deep breaths…well, I guess that won't help you. But you can tell yourself you're fine and try to focus on other things. It helps, really."

"I'm a vampire. I'm not claustrophobic," I grumbled.

"Obviously," said Bria sarcastically.

"All right. Are you able to continue, Alexandre? You could wait at the mouth of the cave if you need to," Selene said, probably meaning to be helpful.

Her comment straightened me up. "I'm fine. Continue." I would be damned if I was going to wait in safety. I could be as hardy as these two.

I followed along, silently doing as Bria suggested. Never in a million years would I admit she was right. However, the self-talk and re-focusing were helping. Fairly soon, the tight aperture gave way to a large room. The tightness in my chest eased instantly. The sound of running water, trickling its way through stone, led us to a small pool toward the back of the cavern. Sparkling minerals crusted the stone walls, casting a luminescent glow of blue and green on the surrounding space. Stalactites and stalagmites jutted up and down all around us. I felt like a caveman in his prehistoric home. Layla's cave of madness also penetrated my thoughts with some sadness.

As we neared the pool of water, Selene cried out, "Something in the water is glowing." She dropped to her knees, her flashlight skittering away.

Bria and I stood overhead, our beams trained on the glowing water.

"Be cautious, Selene," I whispered.

Having been a witness to river demons and the god of death, I would never look at anything as innocent again. For all we knew, this pool could be filled with acid or invisible vampire-eating parasites.

Selene touched one index finger to the surface of the water. Nothing happened. She dipped in her fingers, held them for a moment, and then plunged in her whole hand. She braced herself on the edge with the other one. She slowly, deliberately, explored the small, shallow pool.

A sharp intake of breath startled me. "I've got something," she said in a barely audible voice.

Selene withdrew her hand with a splash, sending water raining down over the front of her clothes. In her grasp was the object from the diagram. It was unmistakable. The amulet glowed a fierce green and was larger than I anticipated, about the size of a golf ball. The rounded handles on either side of the stone would be easily accommodated in my large hands.

"Put it in my pack, Alexandre, and let's get out of here. I'm starting to get a weird feeling. This was too easy." Selene raised her hand, passing me the stone.

I snatched the amulet and jammed it in Selene's bag. As I secured the all-important object, an odd sound reached my ears. It was almost like tapping, a lot of tapping, and it was getting louder. So, she jinxed us, after all. I wanted to point this out, but it hardly seemed the time.

"What is that?" Bria's words rushed out. She swept the room with her light as Selene jumped to her feet.

Bria's light fell on the stone wall to our right. We saw them at the same time. Hundreds of spiders, the size of my head, were streaming from a crack at the far side of the room. The beige of the stone was becoming a solid black with hundreds of arachnid bodies. Only they weren't staying put, they were coming toward us. If we stood there any longer, they would have us pinned in the back.

"Go!" I shouted.

Selene took off, but Bria seemed frozen to her spot. She didn't move. I snatched her up, knocking her light from her hands as we flew with inhuman speed back toward the small tunnel where I had panicked before. Demon-hunting Bria apparently drew the line at enormous spiders.

I held her close to me as I darted through the opening. She was limp and quiet until one of the diabolical demon insects landed half on the back of my neck, half on Bria's hand. She shrieked so loudly, I thought she might cause hearing loss for the both of us.

"Brush it off, Bria!" I yelled, not wanting to drop her or lose my momentum.

She whimpered audibly, not moving her hand. A second later, something hot pierced my flesh.

"Get it off, dammit!" I hollered again, not very gentlemanly. She moved her hand and pushed it off me.

"The damn thing bit me," I said as we emerged into the mouth of the cave.

"Sorry," she choked out.

Selene was already in her harness. "Give me Bria, there isn't time."

Bria jumped out of my arms and sprang onto Selene's back. In a moment, they were gone, out of harm's way. Still moving, I swiped my hand along the back of my neck, feeling the moisture there. Whether it was blood or venom, there was no time to investigate. I didn't think charmed spiders could kill me, but I didn't want to find out.

Instead of reattaching to my harness, I launched myself out onto the side of the cliff. The scurrying of the gigantic spiders had reached a fever pitch, and I knew there was no time to lose.

I slid down about ten feet before finding a good hold. Using my preternatural strength, I scaled the face of the cliff. Finding handholds was easily done once I had the hang of it. I sprang from crevice to crevice like a hound from hell. I expected the unnatural spiders to continue their pursuit, but once I reached the top and peered over, they were gone.

"Enchanted in some way," said Selene, behind me. "My guess is they can't survive outside the cave."

"Thank God for small favors," I muttered, not convinced and still looking over.

"Oh, gross. Don't move," said Selene. I heard the tear of fabric. She began wiping the sticky wet mess off my back with the cloth, flinging a slimy, yellow foam on the ground. "It looks like your body is rejecting the venom. It's oozing out...and there's a lot."

It was then I heard a sound I hadn't heard in centuries; someone vomiting.

"Oh, Bria. It's okay." Selene finished with me and went to her friend.

"I hate spiders so much," Bria said, her voice quaking.

I stood and went over to her. "We all have something, don't we?" I spoke gently, laying a hand on her shoulder.

She looked up at me, her face pale and sweaty, and smiled. "I guess so."

"We'll take our time getting back. Want to hop on?" I asked her.

"Actually, walking would do me some good. At least for a bit." Bria took a bottle of water from her pack. She rinsed out her mouth and then took a long drink.

I helped her to her feet, the three of us strolling toward home. I felt we were accomplishing so much; we had defeated the river demons and taken the amulet that would put the destruction of Balor to an end for another thousand years. The three of us working together were succeeding. We were on the right track and we would prevail.

A.D. BRAZEAU

CHAPTER ELEVEN

"I'm starving." Bria walked unsteadily into the kitchen, making a beeline for the refrigerator. "Toast sounds amazing." She pulled out the butter, then snatched the bread out if its box, dropping it next to the toaster with a soft thud. She moved slowly, her pale face betraying her still queasy stomach.

We had alternated piggy-back rides with walking. She rode on my back until she started to feel sick, at which point she would tap on my shoulder. Bria would then dismount, walking with one hand placed gingerly on her belly until it was calm enough to ride again. It took us a long time to get back and was now close to dawn.

"Sit down, I'll get it," I said, taking her gently by the shoulders and steering her toward the table.

"I'll be examining the amulet in the weapons room, where the light is better." Selene popped her head in the kitchen and then swept off down the hallway.

I slid two slices of bread in the toaster before pouring Bria a tall glass of water. "Drink this. I'm sure you're dehydrated, so no coffee for you tonight."

She took the glass and sipped gingerly. "Thanks. I never do that, you know. It's true I don't like spiders but seeing that…venom." She began to look green again. "That's what did me in."

"Don't worry about it. I'm just glad the critter bit me and not you."

Our eyes met in a way that left me feeling suddenly awkward. I walked the five feet back into the kitchen, turning my attention to gather a plate, knife, and a jar of jam. The counter still had not been wiped clean of several days' worth of old crumbs. Wetting a dishcloth, I mopped up the area while I waited for the bread to toast.

"How are you doing, Alexandre? I'll admit I'm a little surprised by your actions since you've been with us. They don't at all go with what I know of you. I know I've made my feelings about your past clear enough."

"I'm surprising myself," I said, my focus now on buttering the warm toast. "And, I'm fine. Being with Selene, working with the two of you, feels very natural. I wish I could have known my sister sooner."

"Oddly, it feels natural for me, too. I admire Selene so much. To live as long as she has and to be dedicated to helping others, to make her immortality count for something, it's special. Selene has such a Zen master-like nature. She's very easygoing. When we first met, she had difficulty accepting help. She had to do everything on her own. She's getting better, though. I couldn't believe she let you pack our climbing gear." She paused, taking a sip of water. "You two had the same maker, didn't you? Selene said she went crazy, wiped out others she had turned." Bria's color was returning as she became rehydrated.

"Yes, we did. Although, we were with Layla at different times. Layla told me she had no clear understanding of where she came from or even how long she had been a vampire. She had a different story for Selene. When I asked her, she said she was born as she was; a fully formed immortal. I knew this couldn't be true as she wasn't fully formed, but rather somewhere in the middle of her teenage years. I wasn't with her long, maybe a year, before I had to leave. I hated to do it, but her madness was too much to bear. One thing I took away from Layla was to never turn a human before maturity is reached."

"Which is why you waited to turn what's-her-name," Bria pointed out.

"Millicent. Yes, I wished to wait not only until she was physically mature, but I wanted her to be emotionally mature, as well. A mistake, as I said, the first in a series. I left Layla to strike out on my own before she sought out Selene. Layla never told me of her plans regarding my sister. Of course, it's possible she didn't know of Selene while I was with her. Layla was beginning to show serious signs of mental distress while we were together. I would find her talking to no one. She often saw things that weren't there. And most disturbing of all; she began to cut herself. Of course, the wounds would heal almost instantly. But to watch her bent over her arm, cutting into it again and again, was horrible. I eventually had enough. There was nothing I could do for her, and our cave began to feel like a prison." I set the toast with its accompaniments in front of Bria.

"Cave? You lived in a cave with her?" Bria helped herself to a piece of toast, slathering it with butter.

I nodded. "Maybe that's where it came from, the panic. Who knows? There was something wrong about that island, Layla's island, I always felt it. The jungle vegetation would have been natural in the Caribbean, but it was oddly out of place in the Mediterranean. Now that I know a little more about enchantments, I'm beginning to wonder if the entire island was magical in some way." I rubbed my hand over my face as I sat down across from a woman who was beginning to feel like a friend. "Now, my turn for a question. Why have you remained as you are? Has Selene not offered you the change?"

This question had been forming since our encounter with the river demons. Yes, Bria was a strong fighter, but she was mortal, after all. Had Selene not taken the blast from Balor's eye, she would now be in the ground.

"She offered almost right away." She stopped to take a bite of toast. "I have no desire to be what you are, no offense," she said, with a full mouth.

"None taken. I thought fighting demons and all, you would want the extra strength." I thought of Annie and her single-minded determination when we first met to become a powerful immortal with the purpose of fighting the English with greater powers.

"It isn't worth the payoff. To live an eternity, possibly turning mad in the end, watching the people around me wither and die while I go on endlessly, drinking blood. It's not for me. I would like to have a life again one day, maybe even one that involves a husband and children." Crisp toast crunched in her mouth as she chewed and talked.

I smiled at her. I couldn't exactly imagine Bria with a baby in her arms, but what did I know? And she wasn't wrong about the rest. Being a vampire had turned me from a man who should have been so much into a worthless, sarcastic, lazy, murdering...well, I could go on. I was too lazy to even go after Octavian after I was changed. I could have ended him in any number of creative ways. After, his power would have been mine, the throne of Egypt would have been mine. I hadn't, I had simply disappeared.

I feared madness, too. Toward the end with Mills and Kathryn, I thought I had gone mad. Something pulled me back, and now, here I was. I still wasn't sure of my worth, or how I would handle the ultimate battle with Balor, but I felt I belonged. Belonging was not something I had truly felt in a long time, maybe not since my mother held me in her arms at the feet of Isis.

"You're not afraid of death?" I asked simply.

She looked at me, seeming to consider the question. "No. I'm afraid of the pain, I suppose. But, not the release itself. I want to defeat Balor. I want to go on, I want to help the people of my land, and do what is right. There is a risk in everything that is worthwhile. Sacrificing my future so others may have theirs and to save so many is worth it. You and Selene may be a lot stronger than I am, but you too are chancing an unseen future." This was far from the brash woman banging on my door in the hallway of the Ritz. I was seeing her more and more for the multi-layered woman she was.

She was right. Balor could easily kill one of us, the children of the gods. Maybe this was what pulled me back from the brink of insanity, the opportunity to offer it all for this moment.

"Eloquently said. I understand you, Bria. Had you spoken those words to me a few weeks ago, I would have laughed you out of my sight. As it is, right now, this night, I understand you." I leaned casually back against the bench, feeling more comfortable than I had yet with her.

"I know. I can see it in you. I keep seeing this sliver of integrity bursting forth, changing you from the villain into a better person. I refuse to say hero, but Selene was right all along. Even knowing what you did, she never doubted you would step up, not really." She paused, draining her glass. "She's kind of annoying that way."

I laughed. "You should probably get some sleep. Although, I'm not telling you what to do." I held my hand up, eliciting a snort from Bria.

"I was already planning on it, after a hot shower." She polished off the last of her toast before getting up to put her dishes in the sink.

I refused to picture her soapy and wet in the shower, so after she left me, I sought out Selene as a distraction. There was another hour to go until I would be blissfully blacking out.

"What else have you discovered about our wonder twin's amulet?" I joined my sister at the metal table in the weapons room, pulling up a stool.

She had a jeweler's eye loupe jammed over one eye, the other squinting over the bright green stone. "Cute. I have learned absolutely nothing. Looks like a jewel, nothing else special about it. Unfortunately for us, I'm not a witch, nor do I know where to find any." She pulled the loupe from her eye and set it down next to the stone.

"What would a witch be able to tell us?" I knew they existed but had never met or even seen one before.

"For starters, he or she could tell us if this is truly an enchanted object. Kind of important to know as we head into battle with Balor. This object could deal the final blow, or it could be a pretty piece of glass. It seems we may not find out until the last moment." She slipped the loupe into a velvet pouch.

"In all your demony travels, you haven't come across any witches?"

She sighed, moving off the stool and stretching her limbs. "Only a couple. Real witches are hard to come by these days. Where they are now, it's impossible to say. Locating them would take time we don't have. They're tricky."

"Why did Lugus choose a cave to hide the stone? Knowing this may give us a clue." I realized the amulet was hidden to keep it away from our demon friends, but couldn't it have been a little easier to find?

"I imagine the cave was chosen because it's an already fortified structure. All you need to do is hide the opening with a spell and you're in business. Set up a couple of other magical enchantments, like the spiders, and you're really good to go."

"Yeah, those bastards alone would be enough of a deterrent to most." I rubbed the back of my neck.

"Exactly. If you're going to hide an enchanted object, it can't be a walk-in, walk-out scenario. Which is why I was having the feeling we hadn't been challenged enough. We should've had our guard up even higher. Lugus was a demigod, as well, he had access to magic. Clues were planted, here and there, which is why we were able to find it, after a lot of research. Lugus would have wanted to keep the amulet hidden from Balor and his minions, but also wanted it found again, when the moment was right."

I picked up the amulet, turning it over in my hands. "Sounds too complicated. I guess all we can do then is have faith this will work."

"That's all we can do," Selene agreed. "You've been a pleasant surprise, Alexandre."

I couldn't help but chuckle. "Funny, another woman recently told me the same thing."

"Yes, well, I believe Bria has found you a tad more surprising than I have. I knew given the opportunity and our bloodline you would rise to the occasion." Selene's warmth shone through her eyes.

"You're probably the first person to have such faith in me. I didn't think I would rise, I was merely curious about you." I pretended to be absorbed in the stone to tamp down the emotion welling within me.

"Curiosity was the initial step. And, I'm not the first person to have faith in you; Cleopatra was."

I jerked my chin up, meeting her eyes.

Selene stood, regarding me kindly. "We were jealous of you; did you know that? My brothers and I."

"Jealous? Why?"

"You were her chosen one, Alexandre. We both carry the blood of our gods, but you were the son of Caesar, the only son Caesar would ever have, and she gave you to him. You were meant to rule everything, and she truly believed you would." Selene leaned one hip against the table, a faraway look in her eye.

"It was so long ago, it's hard sometimes to hold on to. I let it go for a long time; who I was, what Cleopatra meant to me."

She refocused her eyes on me, unrelentingly. "You did let it go for far too long. You don't know how happy it makes me to be reunited with you, to see the change, this true change, working in you. I was afraid you would disappoint me, the way you were. You're proof that it's never too late, Alexandre."

I stood up with my back straight. "I'm not Alexandre

anymore, Selene. I think we both know that."

She smiled, blood tears forming in her eyes. "Who are you, if not Alexandre?"

"I'm Caesarion," I said, loud and clear.

My sister rushed into my arms. "The King of Kings," she whispered into my ear.

CHAPTER TWELVE

The night was lovely, the breeze from the countryside cool but not cold. I opened the kitchen window to let in the delicious air. Crickets chirped under the cover of darkness. After the cave of horrors, the previous evening ended nicely. I felt happy, truly happy. This was a night to enjoy with a casual stroll. Such simple pleasures were on hold, and we still had a blight to eradicate.

"Selene told me we're no longer to call you Alexandre?" Bria practically hopped into the kitchen where I was preparing her coffee. She looked incredible in tight jeans and a snug white wool sweater.

Her bare feet padded across the floor. She scrunched up her face, freckles bunching together around her nose. "Wait, who are you making coffee for?"

"Mostly for you, but I also needed something to do. You look much improved." I scooped coffee from the tin, dumping it into a filter.

"Yeah, well, we don't have to keep talking about it. Whoa," she squealed, moving next to me and grabbing my hand. "That's way too much. Move aside, Caesarion, and let a peasant handle the coffee." Her sparkly eyes met mine, a playful smile on her lips, our hands still touching.

I couldn't help but smile, too. We continued gazing at each other for a beat too long. I moved my hand away, feeling awkward. Bria would be the death of me next. I was already feeling too much. Thoughts of her crowded in on me while I had lain down this morning. No matter how I tried to push them away, images of Bria almost overwhelmed my mind. I liked this woman, a lot.

"I'll leave this all in your capable hands." I moved around her, wondering what else I could find to fill the hours this evening. It was probably best if I spent time away from Bria.

Selene wanted to do a little investigation into our amulet before we went looking for trouble. I didn't see what good it would do and was ready to act. She couldn't verify if the stone was enchanted. Nothing else seemed to be gained by reading her ancient books.

"You could pop some bread in the toaster for me. If you don't mind." Bria pulled a mug from the shelf, her back to me.

I did as she asked, reaching into the bread box. "Do you ever eat anything else?"

"Sometimes."

I knew enough about women to know her feelings for me were shifting, maybe even becoming confused. I felt something when our hands met, but my feelings were as jumbled as hers. My track record with women was repetitive; meet, seduce, leave. Simple and uncomplicated. In the past, my reasoning was to keep myself free and available should Mills ever come around. I wanted to seduce Bria, of course, but I also wanted to know her.

I pulled out the bread, untwisting the top as I turned back to the island. While I was engaged in this task, I collided with Bria, knocking her off balance. The bread fell from my grasp as I reached out to steady her. She pitched forward, hands tumbling onto my chest.

My hands gripped Bria's upper arms. Her hair, along with the maddening scent of orange blossom, brushed my chin. Instead of pulling back, as I expected her to, Bria lifted her face to mine. My useless breath caught in the back of my throat.

"Are you all right?" I breathed, hooded eyes looking down at her.

She didn't speak or move, only continued to look into my eyes. I felt myself beginning to harden against the cotton fabric of my pants one second before she pushed herself up on her toes, meeting my mouth with hers. Never had I such little control over my erection. I turned my hips slightly to the side, so as not to press it against her.

Her warm hands moved around my neck. I pressed one hand into the red tendrils of her thick hair, balling it up at the back of her head. She moaned softly into my mouth as my lips parted hers, my tongue moving gently inside.

I wanted to thrust her supple body against the counter and ravish her without mercy. But I held back, uncertain what to do for the first time in my life. When I felt my self-control teetering, she pulled away. The old me would have followed up the kiss with some teasing banter, but I didn't want to charm Bria in that way. She stepped back, holding her hand to her lips, eyes trained on the ground.

"I shouldn't have done that," she whispered.

"I'm glad you did," I responded, wanting her to look at me. She didn't.

"I want to like you, Al..." she started, then stopped herself. "Caesarion, you're so likable, so kind since you've been with us. Then I think on your past and I feel contempt well up inside me. I don't know if that's something I can ever make peace with."

I slumped against the counter behind me, feeling defeated. "It's your choice to make. All I can do is live my life." I turned to leave, then paused. "I understand your hesitancy. I hope as we move forward, you consider how much I've changed, and how much better I want to be, because of the influence of you and Selene."

"I've never seen anyone change so vastly in so short a

time. You can't blame me for being wary. Plus, we would never work, anyway. I'm looking for something you can't give me, and I will never be what you are. It's doomed."

I remained turned away from her, glad for it. I was sure my face would betray my anguish.

"I'm sorry to be so blunt, Caesarion. You understand, don't you?"

I nodded, my back still to her. The sound of her voice filled me with pain, more pain than I thought possible. "I do. You should have what you want, Bria, and you will, I know it. Your feet will bring you where your heart is," I said, turning to give her a reassuring smile.

She smiled back. "Look who's using my proverbs. Well done." The sadness in her eyes betrayed her smile.

Without another word, she went back to the coffeepot, swallowing away any feeling or desire she must have felt. I left the kitchen. How could I bear to be near her now? I returned to my small room with the low ceiling and sweet, rustic furnishings with a mission in mind. One that promised a good distraction. Doubtless, Annie had told Mills of our meeting in the streets of Annecy telepathically as soon as it happened.

Even though I reassured Annie I had no intention of further disrupting their lives, I did wonder if they were on heightened alert since the incident. A little vindictive part of me may have even hoped they were worried about what I would do.

I now felt as part of my rebirth, I wanted to fully make peace with the past. This had nothing to do with Bria. What I would do now was for me alone. So, I decided to pen two letters; one to Annie and one to Mills, to not only ease any anxiety they may have, but to apologize, for what it was worth. They could accept or not, that was their right, but at least I would know I had done my best.

There was no fine stationery to be had in the cottage, so I made do with notebook paper. I had a chuckle imagining Mills opening her letter to find cheap lined paper instead of the finest quality French stationery. Since hers would be the most difficult for me, I began with Annie.

My dear child,

Your loud, spirited laughter is greatly missed, as is your calm, levelheadedness and reliable companionship. I never said it much, and I know you felt I didn't always care for you, but I love you, Annie. I always will, no matter how you may feel. You often brought a lightness to our home when Millicent was lost in a bout of depression. You were a good friend to her, always, and for that I thank you. I know what has befallen you since the plantation house, and I couldn't be happier. Not only did you find your love, you put down a detestable being who should have been snuffed out long ago. I'm very proud. No doubt you think I too am a detestable being. Perhaps I am. Much has happened to me in these last weeks, and my hope is, one day, you too will be proud of me. Take care of yourself, my dear. Please know I hold no ill will over the event in Georgia. You did what you felt you must. I will always be your maker, Annie. As such, should you ever find yourself in need, I'm here. Much love, Caesarion. P.S. One day I'll explain.

I couldn't bring myself to sign as Alexandre. Annie would recognize the handwriting. What she would make of the signature, I couldn't say.

Next came the more difficult moment. I put the pen down to regather my thoughts. With slow deliberateness, I folded Annie's letter, slipped it into an envelope, and addressed it to her, care of Mills at the new chateau. Mills would get it to her, wherever she was.

Before I could pen a letter to Millicent, I went to the closet to retrieve my backpack. After reacquiring my head at the plantation, I returned briefly to our Savannah home. The house was quiet, its occupants gone on to new adventures. I remained there for weeks, lost in despair, contemplating what to do next. That Mills would eventually sell it, I had no doubt. What would compel her to return? Her new life would be lived somewhere far away. I half expected an agent to come by to stick a *for sale* sign out front, or movers, come to box up the household goods. But no one came. I was left to think about my actions, on where I would go from there. I often sat on the blood-stained couch, wallowing in my self-pity. Before I moved on, I allowed myself one sentimental token.

On the eve of our departure from France, more than two centuries ago, I gifted to Mills a platinum-caged, blood-red crystal chatelaine perfume bottle filled with her favorite lavender fragrance. On the bottle's cage sat a fleur de lis, front and center. I held the bottle now in my hands, stroking the symbol for France with my thumb. The liquid was used up long ago, but the scent remained. It had wounded me to find it left behind. The sentimentality over the object had been all mine. I closed my eyes, an image of my former love fixed behind my lids. I found she felt dimmer somehow. Perhaps this meant I was truly moving on, moving toward something or someone else. I also pulled out Cleopatra's bracelet; the gold snake coiling its way around an invisible arm. I set both objects in front of me.

Millicent, where do I even begin? Do I begin with I'm sorry? It seems as good a place as any. I don't expect forgiveness, nor do I expect acceptance, but I do need you to know. You and your friends have nothing to fear from me. I won't be striding back into your life. Our past was a mess, which seems an understatement. I do so very much want you to be happy. I won't say I miss you. I won't say I miss talking with you over books in your girly library. I won't say I miss the scent of lavender all around me. I won't say I miss the nights you came to me as a distraction in your grief. These things do not matter. What matters to me is that you go on, that you live, that you smile. Maybe one day you can think of me without hatred in your heart, and only friendship. Forever, Caesarion.

I reread Millicent's letter. I wanted to say more but couldn't put all I was feeling into words that seemed adequate. The note was simple, to the point. Mills was always a person who appreciated the succinct.

I figured these letters would give my girls enough conversation fodder for months to come. The name I signed with would be enough to make them wonder. Imagine if I would have signed with *The King of Kings*, they would never get over that. They would have thought my ego had finally, and completely, taken over my personality.

Once I had them stamped and addressed, I trotted my notes out to the box. I stopped to gaze up at the sky, taking in the stars overhead. Scents of fresh grass and clean air pervaded my senses. I was smiling to myself, feeling lighter than I had a right to when a rustling sound caught my attention.

Looking toward the hedgerow along the side of the house, I expected to see a feral cat or maybe a lost dog. When nothing presented itself, I turned back toward the house. Then I saw it and I froze. A hand, gray and twisted, rested on the grass beneath the bush. This was enough to stop me in my tracks, but there was more. The greenery concealed the body, but I could now hear its breathing, like an infant with a stuffy nose. Once my ears picked up the first one, there seemed to be congested breathing all around me.

Whatever it was, it wasn't alone. I telepathically alerted Selene to danger as I shot toward the door, slamming it and sliding the bolt into place. Hopefully, the little elfin door was a solid one.

"What is it?" Selene threw me a sword.

"No idea. I'm new to this, remember?" I backed up a few paces, planting my feet in a ready position.

"Lake Fomori. I saw one slither past the kitchen window like the creep it is." Bria entered the room, a kitchen knife clutched in her hand.

At the same moment I looked toward her, something from my nightmares crashed through the front window. Glass exploded, shards raining down with a loud tinkling sound. I wasn't expecting that.

"Come on!" Selene yelled over the din.

A.D. BRAZEAU

CHAPTER THIRTEEN

"What the hell is a Lake Fomori, and which lake did it come from?" Realizing after I asked, this was the type of creature that killed Bria's father. The closest lake was the one Selene and I had recently been to. Thoroughly confused, I followed Bria and Selene toward the back of the house, but I didn't make it far.

By the time my feet crunched through the last of the broken glass, something encircled my ankle like a snare, yanking my leg back. As my lower appendages flew backward, the top of my body fell forward. I hit the floorboards with such force, I swear one of them cracked. This could also have been my rib.

Long spiny fingers pulled me toward it, working me as you would a rope. This was the opposite direction I wanted to be moving. I simultaneously kicked with my feet as I clutched at the coffee table with my hands. I rolled onto my back, lifting the table over my head.

The demon was fast. Why did they all have to be so fast? It crawled its way up my body. As I positioned myself to slam the table onto its back, I saw it clearly for the first time. It was a creature low to the ground, with limbs twice as long as its body. The limbs splayed out like those of a stick insect. Its flesh was the dark gray of ash, and it smelled. It smelled like rot and insects, exactly like the underside of a rock. I brought the table down on its back, kicking it off me, as Selene grabbed my shoulders, hauling me to my feet.

We made it to the weapons room, the sounds of more glass breaking and wood splintering outside. As soon as I cleared the threshold, Bria slammed the door with a whooshing thud. She slid two enormous bolts, then turned a large dial, something I associated with submarine hatches, locking us in.

"I didn't know the door was reinforced like this." I stooped to brush invisible germs off my pant legs. Why were all demons so gross?

"This space doubles as a panic room. The walls and floor are reinforced steel. Selene had it installed right after she bought the house. Essentially, we're in a ventilated box. Not ideal for long, but they shouldn't be able to get to us while we regroup." Bria scooted into a desk chair, turning on a computer to reveal live feeds from all over the house. I noticed there were some strange new implements on the steel table, along with something that looked like our amulet. I made a note to ask about this later.

There appeared to be five of the larger-than-life, stick-insect intruders. Two were now upstairs, two remained in the living room, and one was destroying the kitchen. They were searching for something it seemed, and not gently. Every room they entered looked like a tornado hit it after about five seconds.

"I have several questions. The first, why did I not know about this room? Second, does someone want to tell me how many kinds of demons there are? Also, what are they looking for?" I asked no one in particular.

"Us," answered Selene, pulling weapons from the wall. "They're blind, go off scent. Our scents are all over the house."

"Completely blind or unable to see well, like Balor?"

"Completely," said Bria, not moving her face from the computer screen.

"Interesting. Okay, so what do we do?" I stood rooted to my spot. I felt essentially worthless.

"We take them out, obviously," said Bria, the snark returning.

"Obviously. Is this usual? Demons attacking a house like this?" I felt these were questions I should have already had the answers to. A study session would be had in my near future. This was more important than whatever was going on with me and Bria.

"No, it isn't. They are typically cowardly, considering they prefer to hit livestock and people who are alone. Balor's influence is all over this." Selene spoke as she took my sword, sharpening it on a whetstone.

She handed the sword back to me, then gave one to Bria, who stood to take it out of the scabbard to check the sharpness on her own.

"The lesser demons are under Balor's control. We must be making him nervous," Bria said as she laid down her naked sword to strap a knife to her thigh.

"Well, I already knew that. But he isn't here? Why not come himself and finish us off?" I reasoned.

"He may know about the amulet. If he's scried recently, he could have seen the location of the amulet has changed. Likely, he doesn't want us all dead until he has it in his possession." Bria spoke as she moved next to the door. There was a lot of uncertainty about what was happening.

"I suggest I take the two in the living room, clearing the way for Bria to handle the ass in the kitchen. Selene, you can take the two upstairs." This was the first time I had taken control. Previously, I had gone with the expertise of my demon-hunting friends, but I was now feeling more adept at this fighting thing. I was also tired of looking clueless.

"Only one for me? That hardly seems fair to the demon." Bria stood with her hands on her hips, no doubt ready to get to it.

"That skittering monster won't know what hit it," I said, my reward a brighter-than-usual smile.

Selene cleared her throat. "Okay, let's do this. Strike first and strike hard. The skin is calcified. Although they will die in the usual ways, you must pierce through the hardened, outer skin. Remember, they can't see, so don't give them a chance to smell you if you can help it. Go." Selene moved to the door, unlocking it and pulling back the heavy slab.

I was out like a shot. One of the rocky-skin monsters had made it halfway down the hall, right in front of me. Selene's beautiful photographs were falling off the wall, hitting the floor with a crash as the giant bug scraped by. Moving like a thoroughbred, I caught it unaware, stomping on its back and pushing the sword through its skull. These things reminded me of the cave spiders, in human form. It was freaky.

With one down, I kept going right over its corpse and into the living room. I heard the footfalls of the women behind me, not hesitating for a second. I pushed any worry I had for Bria out of my mind to focus on the task at hand. She could handle herself, and she wouldn't appreciate me watching out for her.

My second creature, having heard the commotion, was already coming for me. I didn't have much time to worry even if I wanted to. It was creeping stealthily across the floor on hands and feet. I paused a second too long and the thing whipped my ankles out in front, once again flinging me onto my back. Not the ideal position when I needed to put all my strength into a sword thrust.

Like its friend, this one too began to crawl its way up my body, scraping its hard, outer skin against mine, the smell of saturated earth almost making me gag. I twisted around, meaning to move him onto my back, so I could thrust it off, but it held me fast. These skinny, slithering devils were stronger than they looked.

I threw my arm up, the sword contacting the side of its face. I managed to slash the charcoal-like flesh, flaking off pieces of rock-like skin, but the injury was not significant enough to stop it. The lake demon continued moving up my chest as I bucked and fought with all my might. I could not dislodge it. As skinny as they were, they were deceivingly strong.

The creature placed its hands on my upper arms, pinning them down to the ground. Its breath was hot, stinking, and the wound I had given it was leaking a foul-smelling sludge which dripped onto my chest in thick glops. I continued thrashing, trying with all my might to fling it off.

Suddenly, I saw a flash of red hair. The red hair disappeared as the lake demon's face came down with a quickness, right over mine. "Don't move."

I froze at Bria's words. A second later, more sludge fell into my face as Bria thrust her sword into its skull, the tip coming dangerously close to piercing my eye.

"You're welcome." I heard her say, somewhere overhead.

I realized the weight of the demon had increased as Bria stood on its back.

"Can you get off?" I murmured, not wanting to open my mouth to the sludge.

Her feet hopped lightly onto the floor, decreasing the weight of the demon by a good bit. I shoved the corpse off my body.

"First venom, and now demon ooze. Lucky you." She snorted.

I moved onto my side, wiping off as much of the ooze as I could onto the floor. "At least I didn't throw up," I parried, suddenly grumpy. Not only was I covered in ick, I was saved by a human.

"Very funny. You'll never get over it, will you?"

Glass shattered overhead, alerting us to the fact that Selene was still engaged in battle. Bria took off for the stairs with me right behind her. We found a dead demon in the hallway, launched ourselves over it, and continued.

The sound of furniture overturning led us into my

bedroom, where we found Selene pinned up against the wall. The demon had her by the throat with one hand, struggling to get her sword from her with the other. I shouldered past Bria, not wanting to be outdone again. My sword sank through the back of the demon's head. After I pulled the sword out, the demon fell to the ground like a sack of dirty laundry.

"Thanks." Selene pushed herself off the wall, tumbling toward the armchair. "Those things reek. We'll never get their stink out of the house, which they've ruined."

"We'll get the smell out. And we'll put the house back to rights. Don't worry. How do we know we won't have other visitors?" She was right about the odor. I was planning on burning my clothes.

"We don't. They could strike again at any time, bringing Balor with them." She made a face as her head fell against the back of the chair. She had a defeated look about her, which I wouldn't allow.

"There isn't much we can do about that except fortify the house and move on to confronting Balor on our terms. As for the mess here, it's only a window, some furniture, and a lot of cleaning. The three of us can handle it, no problem. You said before, we must be making Balor nervous. That sounds like a good thing to me. It means he'll be off balance, not sure what to expect. All things that will help us defeat him. Now get up, we have work to do."

Selene groaned but used the arms of the rose-printed chair to push herself to her feet. "Bria, can you start in here? It's probably the least damaged room. Caesarion and I will start with the window. It's important we get that secured as soon as possible."

Bria saluted, making Selene laugh. "All right, you two. Let's do this."

CHAPTER FOURTEEN

Cleanup went well. Selene and I secured the window with wood from the cellar, along with several pieces of wood from the broken furniture. It was a bit of a hodgepodge, but it would work until the glass could be replaced. While we were busy with our task, Bria swept shards, tossed bits of furniture into the outdoor bin, and her favorite; mopped up demon sludge. Selene's spirit improved as we worked.

After the house was in order, Selene told me to come with her to the weapons room. It was then I remembered the instruments I saw earlier.

"What's all this stuff?" I bent over the table. What I saw was what looked like crafting supplies.

"You tell me. What do you think of this?" Selene held up an object which resembled our amulet, minus the stone.

"The metal is obviously new, not aged like ours, but the shape is dead on. What's it for?"

Selene held up a piece of green glass, shaped like a diamond. "As soon as I fix this into the center, we will have a replica, which we'll use to fake out Balor. It only needs to hold his attention long enough to pull him a few steps away from the veil."

I took the fake gem from her, turning it over in my hand. I thought, in the right light, it could work. "Good job. Where did it all come from?"

"Bria had an artisan metal worker in the village over make the symbol and setting before we even had the original in hand. I ordered the jewel from the Internet. The overnight shipping was worth the forty bucks."

I laughed. "It certainly was." I pulled up a stool as Selene turned on a small, brand-new soldering iron. "Do you know how to work that?"

"Of course, that's what manuals are for. A little glue, a little solder, and *voila*."

I was glad to see the setback of the evening had not dampened her spirits for long.

The events of the evening had eaten up most of our dark hours. We used the remainder of the night to put together our replica. Selene gave me a list of household ingredients and where in the house to find them. She used vinegar, hydrogen peroxide, salt, and degreaser to add a patina to our new metal. In the end, I thought it would work perfectly.

The next evening, I woke to a knock on my door.

"Come in." I propped myself up on the pillows, pulled the sheet down to my waist, and hoped it was Bria on the other side.

Instead, Selene pushed the door open, holding the knob in one hand. "I'm going to be gone for a bit. The fight is coming. I'm thinking tomorrow night. I want Bria to rest and I need to feed. I've been neglecting myself. Want to join me?"

I shook my head. "I'm good. And we probably shouldn't leave Bria alone." As I sat, I was careful to keep the lower half of my body covered.

Selene laughed. "Yeah, because she's so helpless. Didn't she come to your rescue last night?" Her smile was wide, playful. We all felt better when Selene was cheerful. Her mood was contagious.

"We've all rescued each other, I believe." I tried to look serious but failed, matching her smile with my own.

"Right. Let's make sure we're being real here. You want to stay close to Bria." When I didn't say anything, she continued, turning the knob back and forth in her hand. "You shouldn't pursue her, Caesarion. I know you've changed, but I couldn't stand to see Bria hurt. If Alexandre decided to show his face again, the aftermath would be brutal."

"I understand, Selene, but I wouldn't hurt her for the world. Honestly." I meant this. I had grown to care for them both dearly in a short time.

"I'll see you later," she said as she pulled the door closed behind her.

I flopped back on the bed, throwing an arm over my face. Selene wasn't wrong. I had changed, that was clear. But what if I became intimate with Bria, and Alexandre returned to love her and leave her? I didn't think that would happen, but I didn't think I'd be fighting demons at this point in my existence either. Bria wanted a life I couldn't give her. Still, staying away would be difficult.

Pretty soon, familiar sounds began to travel up from the kitchen; the tinkling of a coffee cup being selected from the shelf, along with the crunch of a scoop diving into a bag of grounds. I sighed, wondering if I should remain in bed for the night. Out of sight, out of mind.

A shout from below propelled me to my feet. "Caesarion, come hang out with me!"

Well, that settled it. Hanging out I could do. I was sure I could even manage to keep my hands to myself. I pulled on jeans and a t-shirt on my way out the door.

"How did you know I was here?" I asked, sauntering in through the kitchen doorway.

"Selene said you were staying. Want coffee?" She filled the pot with water.

"Sure, but I'll take mine with blood." Her hair was freshly washed. I could smell the citrus of it from across the room. Desire rose up in my body.

"All out," said Bria, not missing a beat.

"Then black is fine." I slid onto the bench, trying to look anywhere but at Bria. I would master these feelings. Friends and work partners, that was all we could be to each other.

"What did you do before all this?" I asked her. This was something I had been curious about for a while. I tried to picture Bria with a day job and couldn't think of anything that suited her.

"I was a school teacher. I taught the wee ones," Bria said, pouring water from the pot into the coffee maker.

"I don't know what I was expecting, but it wasn't that. A teacher? I'm assuming your style of dress was a little more...conservative. Not so tight and battle ready?"

She snorted. "You would be surprised to know my wardrobe contains as many modest dresses as it does skin-tight pants. I'll gladly be returning to my life after we finish here."

I rather enjoyed the skin-tight pants. I scowled, looking out the window to avoid further commentary about the normal life she craved. She must have noticed my discomfort because she asked, "You okay? Need an Irish proverb, do ye?"

I chuckled, shaking my head. I focused on my hands as I willed myself to think of demons, ancient texts, rock climbing, anything but Bria.

"What is it, Caesarion?"

I looked up to see Bria was now standing much closer. I could reach out and pull her to me without moving anything but my arm. "How did you manage to sneak up on me?"

The coffee pot began gurgling, spluttering steam on the counter. The rich scent of Columbian roast filled the air. Bria stood, one hip against the end of the counter. She still hadn't spoken. She stood there waiting, as if she knew I had something on my mind.

"It's nothing." I paused, rubbing at my eyes. "That's not true. It's you and my feelings for you."

"You have feelings for me? I thought I irritated you to no end." She was joking, probably trying to lighten the mood, but she knew. She had to know after the kiss we shared.

"You do irritate me. I shouldn't have brought it up." I moved to stand with every intention of leaving the room. Maybe I would go find Selene and rip something's throat out. I was sure there was a rogue demon or two nearby.

Bria surprised me by moving in front of me, placing a gentle hand on my arm. "Wait. I have feelings for you, too. Feelings I'd rather not have, truth be told. It's not like anything could come from this, Caesarion. I've already told you, I will never allow myself to become what you are. But I cannot deny how powerfully attractive I find you." She looked up at me, searching my eyes with hers. For the first time, I noticed the specks of reddish brown throughout her eyes. They matched the freckles dusted across her cheeks and nose.

Boldly, I moved my hand up to her face, brushing her hair back behind her shoulder. As I brought my hand back down, she caught it, bringing it back up to her face and laying it against her cheek. She turned her mouth to my palm, kissing the soft flesh and igniting a flame within me.

I moved my other hand around the back of her head, turning her face to mine and bringing my mouth down upon hers. She was unrelenting, which I wasn't expecting. Bria met the force of my kiss with equal measure, pressing herself fully against me. I immediately went hard.

As we kissed, Bria slid a hand down my chest until her fingers lightly brushed my hard penis through the fabric of my jeans.

I sucked in a breath. "Are you sure?" I breathed, barely breaking the kiss.

"I have to have you," she said.

I closed my eyes, pressing my lips more firmly against hers. Sweeping her up in my arms, I wasted no time getting us to my room.

Once inside, I laid her gently on the bed, moving my body on top of hers. I needed the contact with her, to feel her underneath me. I pulled back only for a moment as she removed my shirt over my head and then wriggled out of her own. She wasn't wearing a bra, and her small mounds were firm, her nipples taut. I dipped my head to take one in my mouth, delighted when she gasped in pleasure.

Moments later, our pants were peeled off, and I was working down her athletic body. I enjoyed a couple of stops along the way. Bria was ticklish. Now and then, my lips grazed her skin, eliciting a giggle, making me smile. She made me feel like a man who hadn't done this thousands of times. This was different in a way I couldn't define. Was this Bria or was it me? Had I so fundamentally changed?

When I finally found myself at her center, I positioned myself between her legs, parting them gently to allow myself access to all of her.

"You're taking an awfully long time to get to the good stuff," she teased, watching me from the pillow.

"Savoring every moment," I said huskily.

Bria smiled, biting her lip with what seemed like anticipation. I lowered my face to tease her with my tongue. She began panting, moving her hips in a small circle. When I knew she was ready, I enveloped her cleft in my mouth, sucking and licking until she came with a violent spasm, crying out. Her hands clutched at the back of my head, pushing me farther into her. Together, we wrung out every drop of her orgasm.

When she was spent, I crawled my way back up her body, Bria breathing hard beneath me. Her mouth met mine as I pushed myself into her. Bria's head fell back, mouth open in pleasure. She tightened her legs around me, guiding my backside with her soft hands.

"Faster," she moaned.

I did as the lady bid until she was crying out a second time, and I along with her. I collapsed next to her, feeling a happiness I'd never known before. I kept this to myself. I only wanted to enjoy this moment with Bria, not bog it down with what-ifs.

She went to the bathroom to clean up, coming back moments later in one of my white t-shirts. Never had my plain shirts looked so good. I wanted her again, but she looked tired. After tonight, along with the last several nights of demon hunting, she had every right to.

"Lay down and sleep." I moved the blankets back for her as she crawled into my bed.

I thought she might want to talk about what happened, but within seconds, she was breathing deeply, asleep. I kissed her on the forehead. I wouldn't disturb her slumber for the world.

CHAPTER FIFTEEN

Waking the next evening, I found the bed empty of my partner. I had hoped to pull her warm body underneath mine but instead was greeted by cold sheets. A sigh of displeasure escaped my lips as I begrudgingly removed myself from bed to dress.

Without Bria, the room felt as raw and mockingly empty as the bed. I needed to be close to her warmth. Humming a tune as I pulled on my jeans, I couldn't help but be amused. Had anyone else the audacity to call me giddy, I would have ripped out their throat, but that was what I was; giddy. I left the room without bothering with shoes, too excited to find Bria. I wanted to pull her into my arms and press my face into her orange-blossom-scented hair.

I couldn't remember the last time I woke happy. Waking in Savannah started to become a drudgery. I never knew how I would find my companion. Would she be in good humor or ill? I stopped, fresh realization hitting me in the face. Mills and her despair hadn't made sense to me. The inability to move on, when all I'd done all my life was move on, was an emotion I could never grasp. But now. Now I did understand her. I wasn't willing to admit I loved Bria but imagining losing her forever felt like a knife to the gut.

At the bottom of the stairs, I heard the voices of the two women who had come to mean so much issuing from the kitchen. Together, their voices sounded like a low, sweet melody. The scent of brewing coffee, one I never much cared for before, inspired a feeling of homey comfort.

Bria and Selene stood side by side, talking with serious faces. I locked eyes with Bria as I moved toward her. She looked away, picked up her mug, and moved to the other side of Selene. To the casual observer, her movement would appear as if she were only interested in refilling her cup. I saw it for what it was. She was distancing herself from me. I tried to tell myself it was Selene's presence which led her to be more guarded, but I knew it was more than that. The look on her face was carefully controlled.

"We need to discuss our next move, Caesarion." Selene was eyeing me through narrow slits. Of course, she knew what transpired and seemed none too happy about it. "I'll meet you two in the living room."

She moved around the counter, eyeing me the whole way. I felt like a child under the reproachful glare of his mother. Cleopatra had the same ability. To cut through to your soul with one glance.

With Selene out of the room, I moved in closer to where Bria now stood, wiping the counter. "Why does it feel like you're avoiding me?" I stood several feet away from her, trying to look nonchalant. I tapped a bare toe on the cold wood floor.

"Last night was lovely, Caesarion. Stress relief we both needed," she said, finally meeting my eyes with her own. "But it can't happen again. We need to focus on the task at hand. Besides, we both know the outcome of this already. Let's chalk it up to a fun night and move on. I'm sorry if this hurts you." She was squirming, moving from one booted foot to the other.

Not wanting to betray my feelings too much, I simply said, "Not a problem. You've made your feelings perfectly clear. And you know me, I'll never turn down an attractive woman."

I didn't mean to sound so derisive, but I knew I did. Turning on my heel, I went to join Selene in the next room. Truth be told, I was stung. Stress relief? If that was all last night was for her, then fine. I could handle it. Call it a taste of my own medicine, if you will. Only one other person had caused me to feel the pain of rejection so acutely, and somehow, this felt worse. I wasn't in love with the woman, I couldn't be. Still, the ache in the lower recesses of my chest and the unusual queasiness in my belly spoke of deep feeling, whether I would admit to it or not.

Why was I doomed to only feel for women who would reject me when there were hundreds, maybe thousands, over the years who would have gladly let me love them? Was it truly the ones who run away are the ones we find the most compelling? This seemed true in my case. Maybe I should swear off women altogether.

The living room seemed darker than it had only moments ago as I had passed through. Perhaps it was only my mood. Selene raised her head, peering around me as I sank into her rose-printed armchair, the mate to the one in my bedroom. I focused on the wood-beamed ceiling.

"I really wish you hadn't, Caesarian," she whispered. "I need you both at full capacity, not fawning over each other or distracted during battle."

"I'm not sure what that means, but don't worry. There's no fawning here. Bria made it clear she was happy to use me last night and that it won't be happening again." I slouched down against the back of the chair, gazing now at the table where Selene had an open notebook and the two amulets.

"Wow, okay." She cleared her throat. "Bria, can you come in here, please," she called out to her friend. I was glad she wasn't pursuing a conversation I had no interest in having.

I crossed my arms in front of my chest, knowing I looked like a forlorn child and not caring in the least. The scent of Bria's coffee cup preceded her as she walked around me to take a seat next to Selene.

"What do we have?" Bria trained her eyes on the table.

"With the attack on the house, things are ramping up. It's time to take the fight to Balor, ready or not. If he catches us unawares again, it may be for the last time." Selene spoke with the authority of a professor, making eye contact with each of us in turn.

"Agreed. I'm all in, Selene. Tell us the plan. I'm ready to get this over with."

I winced at Bria's words. Thankfully, no one was paying me any mind.

Selene leaned forward, pulling the notebook into her lap. "The plan is simple. Bria will draw out Balor, acting as bait, using our dummy amulet. We need him far enough away from the portal for me and Caesarion to slip in behind him, cutting off his access. When he turns back to us, we'll be holding the real amulet between us, which will then be activated by his gaze. The blaze from his eye will bounce back from the stone and give us the power to turn him, pushing him back behind the veil and sealing it."

"What if he looks at one of us before the stone? We'll be incinerated." Death by fire seemed inevitable for at least one of us, a sure way to kill an immortal. I refused to squirm, knowing Bria had me fixed in a sideways gaze.

Selene closed her eyes for a moment and then gave a small shake of her head. "Supposedly, as long as we are gripping the sides of the amulet, we'll be shielded."

"Supposedly?" I questioned. Supposedly didn't seem like enough to go on.

"Yes, there is no way to test it, except in battle." Selene closed her notebook, folding her hands over the cover.

"I'm not ashamed to say I don't like your plan one bit, Selene. There are too many variables. What if the amulet doesn't work the way you expect? And, you're assuming he'll be alone, without his minions surrounding him? That seems rather naïve for an experienced demon hunter." I knew I was contradicting myself but was feeling salty after being dumped. I also didn't relish the thought of being burned alive.

"Hey," snapped Bria, only now giving me her full attention. "Don't speak to her that way. She's not assuming anything when it comes to Balor. He most likely will be alone, that's how he fights. He may send his minions on raids, but when faced with a battle, he takes it on himself. And, the amulet…well, Selene has done her best to figure it out. She can't do anything about the fact that there isn't much to go on. You were good with all this the other night."

I threw my hands up in mock surrender. "Fine. Count me in for the suicide mission."

Bria pulled a face, rolling her eyes for good measure. "That's not what this is. If Selene thinks the amulet will shield you, it will. Besides, I think we all knew, at least Selene and I did, that we may not make it out of here."

I was having a hard time remembering why I signed on for this. I opened my mouth, not quite ready to give in, but Selene cut me off. "And there's one more thing."

"Oh, great. I can't wait to hear it." I crossed my legs, settling in for the story.

Selene ignored my immature comment. "The final moment will require a sacrifice."

"A sacrifice?" Bria asked, her voice suddenly small, her previous fire dying out. "What does that mean?"

Selene sighed, shaking her head. "Again, I don't know. I'm as frustrated as everyone else. According to two different texts, when Balor's gaze strikes the stone, something must be given, something big. They don't say what, only that the decision apparently has to be made at the moment for the biggest impact."

"Like a life? One of us has to sacrifice our life without fighting? Just give it up?" Bria suddenly seemed cold as she set down her mug and wrapped her arms around herself.

"Maybe," said Selene. "This Gaelic text makes it clear the choice cannot be made ahead of time. For the decision to have any power, it must be made then and there." Her voice was sad, defeated. "It doesn't seem fair, does it?"

"When is anything ever fair, sister?" Well, I supposed after coming this far, there was no going back. I shrugged my shoulders. "We will do what we must, together. And we will succeed, together." I leaned forward, my face set with determination.

"You're right," said Bria. Removing her arms from her body, she reached for me with one hand, and for Selene with the other. I may have been stung, but I wouldn't snub the gesture. Three unlikely companions grasped hands, forming a circle. More importantly, we were making a pact.

CHAPTER SIXTEEN

As it was still early in the evening, we prepared to set out. There was no putting this off any longer. We outfitted ourselves in our usual fashion, the two amulets being the only addition. Selene carried the all-important genuine article, clipped securely to her belt by one handle. Bria tucked her replica in the back band of her jeans.

During a brief moment, I found myself alone with my sister. "You were right about Bria. We shouldn't have…"

She waved her hand. "It's fine. You're both adults. I was afraid Bria would be the one hurt, should anything happen between you. It looks as if I was wrong."

I looked up into her soft, knowing eyes. I smiled, a tinge of sadness behind my eyes. "Who would have thought it? Selene, I want you to know something before we go out there, facing this uncertain future. The thing with Bria aside, I've never felt more at peace with myself. Thank you for bringing me here. I'm so grateful for the time I've had with you."

"I'm grateful, too. I brought you here, as you know, to use you in this fight against Balor. But during this time, getting to know you, seeing you grow has meant so much. I'm proud to call you my brother." She paused, looking down at the katana gleaming in her hand. She returned it to the sheath on her back. "What will you do about Bria?"

"I'm not sure what you mean, as there isn't much I can do. She is free to make her choice, and I will respect that. No more killing of lovers for me. No more killing of any innocents for me."

Selene met my eyes then, her own crinkled in the corners by a sweet smile. I knew what she was thinking, because I was thinking it too. The transformation was complete, the circle closed. Even if I continued to use the name in the future, Alexandre was long gone, never to return.

"Let's go, guys," Bria called from the living room, breaking the moment.

The way to the portal was an easy sprint. Bria didn't wait for my offer to carry her. Selene moved her sword into her hands, and Bria hopped onto her back as soon as we were outside. I had hoped to say a sentimental word to her, as well, but she wasn't going to give me the chance.

The ground was slick with the intermittent rain from the day before, which made me a little nervous again. We needed all the advantages we could get. Wet soil and slippery grass would not benefit us. It would've been another lovely night for a leisurely walk, not a battle with evil. The evening was alive with my favorite sound of crickets. The fields were dotted with glow worms winking in the night. The recent rains left the air fresh and leafy. I hadn't thought much of where I would go after this. If there was an after to be had, Ireland was surely a place I could be happy.

We approached the mound cautiously, Selene and I flanking Bria. Nothing was about. The portal was in the center of a Neolithic stone circle. The outer stones were just tall and wide enough to hide me if I crouched. Our plan was to take cover behind the two taller stones which flanked the gateway while Bria drew out our foe. Selene said I would be able to detect the shimmer of the veil with my naked eye, due to my lineage, and she was right. The closer we came, the clearer the shimmer appeared.

I could see why the demon portal was called the veil; it was silvery, gauzy. I couldn't believe such a gorgeous sight could be the entryway to a place of nightmarish horrors. It looked like the entrance to a Celtic wonderland.

"It's so easily accessible. How do mortals not fall through?" I asked Selene, telepathically.

"Unlike the enchanted cave, only demons and gods can cross over. It isn't visible to humans nor can they cross," she answered.

The glow was so bright, so vivid, I found this hard to believe. But Bria had told me the same thing. Demon hunter that she was, not even she could see it. At least humans were protected from accidentally walking through the gateway. I can't imagine what a shock it would be to be walking in such a lovely place one moment, then sucked through a portal, into a hell dimension the next.

"It's beautiful," I murmured, more to myself than anyone. The glimmering partition reminded me of a colorless aurora borealis, a phenomenon I saw only once, centuries ago.

"Get into position," Selene whispered.

She and I parted, taking up our places behind the tall, vertical stones, along either side of the veil. Bria stood; back straight, head up, sword gripped in her right hand, a few yards in front of the portal. If I had a breath, I would have been holding it in anticipation.

Balor could smell human flesh. As Selene described it to me, he was unable to sniff out Bria during our previous encounter because Selene's burns had mingled with the scent of his own charred flesh, obliterating all other smells. With all my lessons, I felt I still didn't know all I needed to. According to Selene, it wouldn't take him long to scent Bria now. I stood stiffly behind my rock, tension tightening every muscle. I wasn't supposed to watch her, but I disobeyed, craning my head far enough so I could see. My eyes didn't leave Bria for a moment. Seconds ticked by, then minutes, then even more minutes. Still, my eyes remained focused on Bria. She shifted her stance, moving her weight from one leg to the other. Her hazel eyes moved from the veil to the stone which hid Selene.

There was a shrug of the shoulders from Bria. The breeze rustled the leaves of the few trees surrounding the mound, along with the long blades of grass, lulling me into sleepiness. As I began to entertain thoughts of giving up, there was a sound.

The sound was that of someone stepping under and through a waterfall. Only it wasn't a waterfall being stepped through, it was the portal. The sound was so gentle, so in keeping with what we could see of the veil. Was its appearance different on the other side; ugly, frightening, loud? A moment later, Balor emerged, gigantic and terrifying. These monsters, Balor, most of all, were so out of keeping with reality, I was still jarred by their sight.

He smelled of something burned, dying. His visor was down. Once he was through the veil, and he had fully scented Bria, he began to raise his hand to his helmet. He seemed to have every intention of burning her where she stood.

Bria held up her free palm in a *stop* gesture. "I have something for you. If you burn me, you'll never possess it."

The beast lowered his hand. A loud, trembling bass issued from somewhere deep inside him. I realized with horror this sound was his laughter.

"What is it, little speck? What could you possibly have that I would want?" His voice was an earthquake, tectonic plates shifting against one another.

"I think you know already. But here it is; the amulet." From her back pocket, Bria pulled forth the dummy stone, holding it in front of her.

I was afraid he would rush her, but Balor didn't move. "Why would you give it to me? You must want something."

"I do. I want you to leave here. Find a new place to terrorize." The calm way she spoke amazed me. Self-possession was not a trait Bria lacked. I didn't think there were many humans who could stand and face what was in front of her now.

Balor was silent for a moment. This was part of our trick. We knew Balor had no control over where the portal was located. We only needed him to move forward a few feet. The question was, would he take the bait?

"Deal," he said, moving carefully toward Bria. Bait taken.

When enough space had opened between him and the veil, Selene and I moved in. She gripped her side of the amulet, holding it up for me to grip the other side.

"Balor!" I shouted once we were in place, both our hands on the stone. He was closer to Bria than I would have liked.

The demon whirled, the metal of his armor clanking as he moved. He was surprisingly fast for a giant one-legged being. "I thought this was a trick. Stupid fools." He turned back toward Bria, but she was already running.

Balor lifted his visor, blasting her in the back. Bria screamed but continued to move. My foot inched forward. All I wanted was to run to her.

"Don't move, Caesarion!" yelled Selene. "This is our only chance."

With her one free hand, Selene threw a small dagger from the sheath at her thigh. She nicked the back of Balor's ropey neck. His head flinched upward, setting tree branches alight in the wake of his gaze. Turning toward us, the laser beam of his eye went right over Selene as if she wasn't even there. Selene was right, we were shielded. This gave us the chance we needed to move the amulet into the stream of fire blazing from his eye.

As soon as his gaze hit the center of the stone, he was in our power. The amulet vibrated nearly out of our hands, but we held on with everything we had. My feet slipped on the wet grass. Somehow, I managed to keep myself from falling. Moving in unison, Selene and I walked, amulet held in between us, around the god of death.

He was locked with us, unable to free his gaze from the

amulet. He bellowed, kicking and pawing at the earth under his feet. It was no use. If none of his followers came to his aid, we had him. We continued turning him until his back was to the portal. Selene and I walked forward, pushing him back toward the shimmering gateway.

"No!" he yelled. His voice had lost some of the strength from earlier. Either he knew this was it, or the amulet was weakening him. Maybe a bit of both.

He fought, pushing against us with all his strength. It wasn't enough. Together, Selene and I were stronger. For the first time in my existence, I felt the true power within me. With a whoosh, he was gone, back behind the veil, his gaze of fire cut off. Almost immediately, the once bright, metallic shimmer began to fade, until all that remained was a dull mist. Our arms went slack, though we continued to cling to the amulet.

"Shouldn't the veil disappear completely?" I asked.

Selene and I remained in the same position, not daring to move quite yet. She kept her eyes trained on the space in front of us. "I thought so…maybe. I don't know. I'll stand here and wait. You go check on Bria."

This was music to my ears. My fear for her had not left me for a moment. I released my side of the amulet to run after Bria.

I found her face-down in the grass. Her flesh sizzled, the meaty smell putrid and sickening. The burn was severe. Although not as bad as Selene's had been, for a human, the burns were life-threatening. Bria's breathing was shallow, broken, her pulse almost nothing. I was thankful she was unconscious.

Without hesitation, I tore open my wrist with my teeth, letting the vampiric blood flow over her wounds. Within seconds, the skin began to repair itself. Bria remained unconscious, as I knew she would for a while. I scooped her gently into my arms and went back to Selene.

I came to a stop behind my sister. "Anything?"

Selene shook her head. "No. It must be closed. We did

it, Caesarion." She didn't sound too convinced. "How is Bria?" Selene turned away from the portal, placing a hand on her friend's forehead.

"She'll live," I said, eyeing the mist behind Selene. This didn't feel finished, not by a long shot.

A.D. BRAZEAU

CHAPTER SEVENTEEN

Back at home, I tucked Bria into my bed, waiting to black out alongside her with the sun. Somehow, this room only felt complete when she was in it. I figured she wouldn't be pleased, waking up next to me but, I didn't really care. She could be as mad as she wanted. What I wanted was her next to me. Feeling her breathing alongside me was all the balm my soul needed.

My anxiety over her had reached unbelievable proportions as I watched her run from Balor. Remaining where I stood took every ounce of inner strength I had. Only the thought of even greater loss kept me from moving; the loss of her life. I realized at that moment all that Bria had come to mean to me.

I was in love with the woman, and I needed her near me now as she slept and recovered. Lying next to her, watching her chest rise and fall with her breath, was calming me in a way nothing had ever done before. She didn't have to be with me. I wouldn't go psycho on her like I did with Mills and Kathryn. Her safety and happiness were all I wanted.

Something still nagged at me, though. Our victory seemed to come all too easily. Yes, Bria had been terribly injured, but that alone couldn't have been the price we were meant to pay. It didn't seem enough. Selene thought her text was clear; a dear sacrifice would have to be made to seal the portal. It seemed plain to me that either Selene or I would have to die. The sun was beginning to rise, cutting off my thoughts before I could grasp anything meaningful.

I woke with a start, flat on my back. The room was dark, but not empty. Turning my head, I was surprised to not only see Bria still next to me, but also watching me.

"Don't get mad," I began. "I only wanted to keep an eye on you." I was sure she could see right through me. My ego, once large enough to fill a galaxy, was in no danger of bruising. I no longer cared only for myself as I once did.

"In a death-like sleep?" she asked, eyes narrowed in what seemed like amusement.

I grumbled, moving up to a sitting position. "Something like that."

I turned away, intending to get out of the bed. Instead, I was surprised when Bria grasped the back of my shirt.

"Damn, if you don't have me all kinds of confused." Her voice was playful. This sounded promising.

Leaning back on one hand, I turned my body to face hers. "Do tell," I prompted.

She sighed, releasing my shirt. "I'm thirty-six years old, Caesarion. I don't have time to fool around with you. I want children, a real life. A home that isn't smashed to bits by demons would be lovely, maybe I'll even wear a damn apron. But, against my better judgment, fooling around with you is exactly what I want to do."

"Would you be naked under the apron?" I couldn't help myself, but at least she laughed.

I smiled at her, a little sadly. Alexandre would be making her scream in pleasure by now. The new me didn't want Bria for the short term. I wanted her forever.

"Then we'd better not. I can't believe I said that, by the way. But I can't fool around with you either. I want you for real, and I won't try to pull you away from your dreams. You should have children if that's what you want, and I hope you do have them. If only I could give them to you." I dropped my head.

Bria sat up, scooting close to me. She took my chin in her hand, lifting my head. "Caesarion, I don't want to hurt you, but I do want you. Now. Let's worry about all the serious stuff later. After last night, I feel a great burden has been lifted from all of us. Let's revel in that for a moment. Would that be enough for you, for now?"

"More stress relief?"

"No. Two people who care about each other."

I looked into her eyes, knowing I could never deny her any request. Warmth bloomed through me as I bent my head to capture her lips with mine. She responded with a passion that took my breath away, figuratively speaking. She must have gotten up to brush her teeth. She tasted like mint and heaven.

Her lips pressed against mine urgently, our mouths opening together. I deepened my kiss, penetrating her mouth. I felt her breath quicken, felt the beat of her heart speeding up with every pass of our tongues.

Bria grasped the front of my shirt, drawing me down on top of her. As she lay back, she drew my shirt off over my head. My mouth found hers again, as I pushed my hand up and under her shirt. She was braless, and I growled as my hand met the firmness of her breast.

Needing more access, I pulled back. Together, we tugged off her t-shirt and panties. Bria pushed me onto my back. Once she had my pants off, she covered my naked body with her own. How I loved the warmth of her. I wouldn't make her cold and dead like me for anything in the world. She was alive, so very alive.

I sat up with Bria straddling my waist, my erect penis stiff against her cleft. Bending my head, I took her taut nipple into my mouth, teasing it with my tongue. She gasped, moving her pelvis closer against me. I trailed a hand down her stomach before I moved it between us. Bria moaned deeper, clutching the back of my hair into fists.

I continued to suck at her nipple as I massaged her cleft, rolling it between my finger and thumb. I had her panting and moaning before I pushed two fingers inside of her. Bria cried out softly, grinding herself into the palm of my hand.

"I need you now," she said, her voice husky as she reached down between our bodies, tenderly grasping my erect penis.

It was my turn to moan. Bria guided me toward her, releasing me as she impaled herself. Reaching around her, I grasped her buttocks. I pressed into her, both of us crying out in pleasure. We moved together, slowly.

I was right on the cusp already. Never had a woman driven me so crazy with desire. Thankfully, I didn't have to hold back long. She was right there with me, thanks to my teasing. She brought herself down with increasing speed until she was arching her spine. Head thrown back, Bria cried out, her muscles clenching and then releasing in a great spasm.

I joined her, almost simultaneously. I held on, not wanting to release her quite yet. Finally, I lay back, pulling her down with me. I rolled over on top of her, my face buried in orange-blossom-scented hair.

"That was great, but I do need to breathe." She laughed, panting hard beneath me.

"Sorry," I said, rolling to the side.

She faced me, kissed the tip of my nose, and said, "Don't go anywhere. I'm going to take a shower."

My wicked smile was bright. "May I join? I could be quite useful with those hard to reach spots."

She looked at me, a smile hovering on her lips. "I suppose so."

After our shower of many more delights, I found myself in the modern kitchen making toast and coffee for Bria. I added a sliced-up apple to her plate. I was sure she couldn't subsist on bread alone. Whether she ate it or not was up to her. She sat in the breakfast nook, looking sexy in my t-shirt and a pair of pink flannel shorts.

I was thankful Selene was hibernating in her room. Bless my sister for knowing exactly when her presence wasn't needed.

"For someone who doesn't want to be a vampire, you certainly keep the hours of one." I placed her food in front of her.

She stirred a heaping spoonful of sugar into her coffee. "Thanks. Not for much longer, now that all this is over."

Try as I might to hide my feelings, my face fell as I sat opposite her.

"I mean…oh, I don't know what I mean, Caesarion. You're the last person I thought I would…" she trailed off, shaking her head.

"I know. It's okay. I'm going to tell you something, Bria. I love you."

Her head shot up, eyes wide. I put up a hand. "I'm not telling you this for any selfish reason, or to manipulate you. I simply want you to know. I don't expect us to walk off into the sunset together. I also realize how short a time we've known each other, so I won't be surprised to see you roll your eyes." I paused, there was no roll of the eyes, no derision from across the table. A partial smile spurred me to continue. "This was not a love-at-first-sight love story, I think you would concur. This is a feeling which has grown. You've changed me, you and Selene. I don't know what would have happened to me if you hadn't shown up at the cabin when you did. You not only gave me a purpose, you gave me a reason to change, to become better. I want you to have the life you want. I would like that life to be with me. If not, I completely understand. I want you to be happy." I reached across the table, grasping her hand in mine.

"I love you, too. I can't promise you anything more than that, right now, but I love you, too."

I squeezed her hand reassuringly. "That's good enough for me."

It was good enough for now, it had to be.

CHAPTER EIGHTEEN

I tucked Bria back into bed with several more hours still to go before sunrise. Something continued to nag at me, and our task felt unfinished. My sister must have felt the same as I found her poring over her texts in the living room.

"Well, it didn't take you two long to reconnect," she said dryly, not raising her head.

"The magnetism can't be helped, dear sister," I said, striding into the room.

Selene chuckled. "Once a Roman, always a Roman."

I took the floral armchair, amused by her comment. "You don't think it's over, do you?" The chair had become my favorite place to sit. I was always a creature who appreciated the opulence of grand homes, fine furnishings, expensive linens, and glittering chandeliers. Now I found myself very much at ease here. This quaint cottage felt more like a home to me after this brief sojourn than the hundreds of years I spent moving from house to house with Mills, picking and choosing only the best.

Selene shook her head, worry creasing her brow. "It was too easy. I feel as if we've only been given a temporary reprieve. I went back to the veil earlier, while you were busy. Its shimmer was brighter, as if it were re-charging somehow.

It's not back to where it was, and I don't believe Balor can cross yet. I do believe to permanently close the portal, one of us must make the sacrifice I mentioned. But what, and how?" I could hear the frustration in her voice.

"We must keep looking. Hand me something." I held out my hand. Figuring out this puzzle was a priority. I felt a little sheepish about allowing my baser instincts to rule the first part of the night.

We spent the next hour going through texts Selene had already devoured a hundred times. I had learned secrets could be hidden anywhere; through obscure symbols, written backward, so the words appeared to be nothing but gibberish, written in code, even written on the inside of the binding. I took the last one from my stack, examining it page by page. This book was one I had yet to ever look through. The pages were thick, three or four times the thickness of a regular book.

Halfway through, I turned a page that seemed thicker, somehow, than the others. I suspected there was something hidden here, but I didn't want Selene to see. I had already decided, once we found the key to the sacrifice, I would be the one to make it.

Selene was enthralled in her current read, so I rose soundlessly and made my way to the kitchen. I selected a tiny, sharp paring knife. Setting the book on the counter, spine flat, I held up the page I wanted to explore. With great care, I sliced it open along its outer edge, creating a pocket. I was right. Inside was a small piece of paper, folded once in half. Clever to use such thick paper for all the book pages.

The words were ancient Gaelic, which Selene taught me to read the first time I helped her in her research. To make the sacrifice that would seal the portal, the lamb would have to stand in front of the veil and speak an incantation. Translated it read as; *I offer thee my gift with all that I am. My life, my soul, my heart is yours to choose.*

So, it seemed we didn't make the choice. The veil did. How much simpler this would be if we had one manual with all the information clearly laid out.

The spell rather reminded me of one of Bria's proverbs. While holding the amulet in two hands, it would absorb the energy of the sacrifice and re-direct the energy at the opening, sealing it off for a thousand years. It didn't seem fair that in a thousand years, someone else would have to make another sacrifice.

The inscription wasn't clear on what the offering would have to be to generate enough energy. I had an idea of what I would like to give. But, ultimately, the veil would make the choice, not me. The amulet needed two gods to fight Balor and send him behind the veil. To seal it, only one divine individual was needed. That person was going to be me, I would be the lamb.

I refolded the paper with the all-important incantation. It was slipped discreetly into my flannel shirt pocket. To make sure Selene wouldn't see the gaping hole in the page and wonder what was in there, I carefully tore the paper out all the way to the binding. Hopefully, this would buy me time, should she pick it up to read.

Then, I returned to the living room. Placing the book on the stack, I said, "Nothing." My face was set in a disappointed scowl.

"I still have half a book to go through. Maybe I'll find what we need here," she said, not looking up. She sat, tugging on an ear lobe. "If not, I don't know what we'll do."

I bent down, kissing the top of her head. Startled, she raised her eyes to mine. "What was that for?"

"Just because. I'm going to check on Bria and think." I smiled, turning to leave the room before she could read my face.

I went upstairs, not to check on a sleeping Bria, but to say goodbye. There was no point in putting this off, the time was now. Waiting wouldn't change what needed to be done, it would only make it harder to do it. The veil was re-opening. I had to save my family, my love, and the people of the Isle.

The sound of Bria's gentle breathing greeted me as I entered the room. The bed looked as warm and inviting as Bria herself. Fighting the urge to crawl into bed alongside her, I knelt on the floor, brushing her long hair away from her face. I allowed myself a moment of indulgence, crouching there, imagining how different life would be if only she could be mine. Truly mine, without constraints, no demon threat lurking in the background.

The love I felt for Mills wasn't a true love, I knew that now. It was a possessive love, which wasn't love at all. I didn't want to possess Bria. I only wanted her happiness, for her dreams to be made reality.

"Goodbye, Red," I whispered before kissing her forehead softly. I wouldn't wake her. I would let her sleep peacefully and wake to a different world, one in which all her fantasies could come true.

Before I left for the veil, I would have to acquire the amulet. The stone lay below me in the weapons room. The only way to get there without being seen by Selene was through the back door.

I raised the window as quietly as possible. Surprisingly, the old tracks were smooth, giving me no trouble. Easily, I jumped from the second-story window and onto the back lawn. I hoped Selene's absorption in her reading would give me the advantage over her preternatural hearing. With the grace of a practiced thief, I opened the back door, unlocking it with the spare key Selene gave me when I arrived. Like a cat, I crept on tiptoes to the door of the room I needed to access.

As Selene was coming and going with her texts, she had left the door open. The stone lay in the center of the metal table, wrapped unceremoniously in a dish towel. I snatched it up, making tracks out into the backyard in no time. The door was locked securely behind me. Only thirty minutes remained until dawn, so I raced the sun to the portal.

I didn't stop until I was on the mound. There was no point in taking in the beautiful, crisp almost morning. No time to notice the dew beaded on the leaves and grass. My time on earth was almost up. There were no minutes left for anything but business.

As I neared the veil, I noticed the shimmer seemed to increase with each step I took. There was no time to lose. This was my moment, the reason I had been given a second chance at life. I wouldn't hesitate. Balor must be stopped at all costs.

A.D. BRAZEAU

CHAPTER NINETEEN

Standing in view of the portal, I held the amulet out in front of me by the handles. The green stone shone prettily, like it always did, but otherwise looked the same. There was a knot in my stomach. I didn't want to die, but that was exactly what I was prepared to do. In minutes, I would either be burned to a crisp by the sun, or the portal would have my soul.

Until now, I had never done anything of value. I lived life as in a dream, a dream with no consequences. Selene and Bria had changed me in a way no other beings ever had. I hoped this sacrifice would allow them the freedom to go on, to live a life without fear of it all coming to an end. I wished my preternatural children well. They would flourish, no doubt. For them, I had no fears.

I fixed an image of Bria in my mind; fierce attitude, sassy mouth, flowing red hair, and eyes filled with love. I held this image as I began to speak the words of the spell over the stone. *I offer thee my gift with all that I am.* I not only articulated this, I felt it. The sacrifice was happily made. With each word, the stone grew brighter.

A sound on the other side of the veil drew my attention. A mad, feral roar could be heard. It was Balor. He knew what was happening and he was coming for me. A shadow began to form on the other side, looming larger, darker with every step he took toward the opening. I sped up the incantation. *My life, my soul, my heart is yours to choose.*

On the last line, the shadow menaced opposite me. The figure laughed, low and deep, shaking the ground underneath my feet. "You think it wants your life? What is your life worth? Nothing. The amulet wants something far greater than your life."

Sparks began to fly as Balor tried to push his way through the veil. This wasn't the gentle emergence of last time. The veil was holding him back, yet nothing else was happening. I hadn't died, the portal remained as it was. *Think, Caesarion.* What did I have worth more than my life? I granted the gods that my life wasn't worth much. What was I supposed to give? I thought the veil would choose, but it hadn't taken what I thought it wanted. A new thought began to form in my mind, taking shape with beautiful clarity.

"I give to thee my most powerful gift."

"No!" The thunderous voice almost sent me toppling off the mound. He knew I had it.

"I give my immortality." I stared directly into the stone.

A great vibration shook me, but I held strong. Surely, giving my immortality would also mean giving my life. I suddenly felt as if my insides were melting. I was hot, feverish. A sharp pain in my chest nearly doubled me over. Another sharp pain was accompanied by the feeling of a beat within; unsteady, skipping, stuttering.

My lungs began to burn. I gasped. Dry, painful air-filled organs long without use. My head reeled. I felt nauseated, dizzy. Still, I refused to release the amulet. Sparks flew around me, burning my skin. Balor was beginning to break through, fighting the veil with all his might.

When I thought I would surely die, that I could take no more, an explosion of green light burst from the amulet and everything went black. Stars danced behind my eyes. My head throbbed.

When I woke, it was in confusion. My first thought was that the lights in my room were on. My eyes fluttered open, only to be squeezed shut again against the glare. I felt warm. Birds chirped in the trees, birds that spoke of morning. It was then I realized the light was from the sun. Its rays were a comfort to my cold skin, not a torment.

I opened my eyes, shielding them with my hand. The veil was gone. Well, not gone exactly. I could still see what looked to be a barely visible mist. It would likely never disappear completely. I knew in my heart it was sealed.

There was no sign of Balor. The fact that I was alive had to mean he was safely where he should be. A pain in the back of my throat alarmed me. There was also a pain in my stomach, along with sensations of a tingling prickle through my limbs. I choked out a sob, moisture spilling from my eyes. I wiped a hand across my cheek; real tears, without blood.

The portal was closed, and I was alive, really alive. The amulet lay next to me, looking none the worse for wear. After the blast of refracted light, I expected it to be in a million pieces. I moved to my feet, wincing from a sharp pain in my left leg. Blood trickled down my jeans, pooling in my shoe. Through the slash in the fabric, I could see a deep gash. The amulet must have hit my leg after it expelled its energy. It took me a moment to realize this wound wouldn't heal itself within seconds. Likely, it would require stitches.

I had a feeling a needle piercing my flesh would hurt, but I laughed out loud. I would have to be more careful with this body from now on. The amulet was tucked in my waistband. I began to limp my way home. I groaned, thinking about the walk of several miles on an injured leg, oozing blood. I removed my shirt and tied it around the wound.

"Ah!" I cried out involuntarily. The painful burning was incredibly unpleasant. At least the blood flow would be staunched.

I knew there was a road to the east, not far from where I was, so I hobbled in that direction, hoping to thumb a ride. As luck would have it, not only did I find the road, I found someone kind enough to stop and pick me up. I felt relieved as I took a seat inside the antique car.

"You all right, son? There's a clinic not far from here, I'll be happy to take you there." The old man spoke in a voice I could barely decipher.

"I'm fine, thank you. I need to get home. I can clean up there. I was hiking and fell over some rocks, that's all." All I needed was to get back to the country house. Everything would be fine once I was there.

Selene would be asleep for the day, but Bria would be up, I knew she would. I stared out at the verdant, green landscape as we made our way down the winding lane. Two thousand years had passed since I last saw sunlight moving across the earth. Almost overcome with emotion again, I had to choke back the tears. This poor man thought I was enough of a mess.

"Is it always so beautiful?" My hand trailed out the open window, heather-scented air blasting me in the face.

The old man shoved the car into a higher gear. "What?"

"Everything." He didn't respond, probably thinking I was suffering from a head injury.

I felt anxiety building in my stomach like a rolled-up ball of twine. We couldn't get there fast enough, but still, I was afraid. Would she want me? Really want me? I wondered if I would be capable of giving her the children she so dearly wanted. Children. Was I, Caesarian, formerly Alexandre, thinking with hope about children?

The old man's car came to a stop in front of the walk. "Nice place," he said, his accent thick.

"It is." I hesitated, suddenly unsure how to proceed.

"Don't worry, son. I'm sure everything will be fine." He patted my hand with gnarled, arthritic fingers.

I turned my head, smiling at the elderly gentleman. There

was goodness everywhere. It took fighting demons and losing my immortality for me to see that. "Thank you. I'm sure it will." I got out of the car and limped my way to the front door.

The pain in my leg was beginning to feel like a dull ache. I marveled at it. As a vampire, I had felt pain many times, but it was quick, as the wounds never lasted long. I knew this pain would likely stay with me several days, maybe longer, as the wound took its time to heal. This was a strange idea to process.

The door was flung open before I could reach it. "What on earth? How are you not on fire right now?" Bria looked frantic, her eyes wide, hair a tangle from sleeping. "I woke up to find you gone…in the morning. What's happened? Selene is blacked out in her room. I had no idea what to do." Her words tumbled out in her panic.

I smiled.

"Have you gone mad? Tell me what's happening." Her voice began to rise.

She slammed the door behind us. Limping into the living room, I fell onto the sofa, propping my leg on the coffee table. "First, can you look at my leg and tell me if you think I need stitches? It probably needs to be cleaned, as well. I don't want an infection and I've no idea how to do these things."

Bria froze in the middle of the room. "Why would you need stitches? Pour some blood over it." She continued to stare. "Why do you look the way you do? You're sweating, you seem paler, but a different kind of pale. Caesarion, what happened? Where did you go?" Her voice became very small, as she remained in place in the center of the room.

"All right, I'll put you out of your misery. I took the amulet and went to the portal. The key we needed, a spell to seal the veil, was found by me, right before dawn. I knew one of us would have to make a sacrifice and I wanted it to be me." I took the amulet from the back of my jeans, then tossed it onto the table with a clang. "I made my sacrifice, sealing the portal. It's finished. I guess we get to hide this thing now."

She blinked. "You're mortal," she whispered.

"I am, and I'm in pain. Can you help me with the leg, please?" Bria continued to stand unmoving before me. "I know it's a shock, Bria. Imagine how I'm feeling. But, please, some antiseptic and a painkiller would be appreciated. I'm not telling you what to do, I'm asking for help." It was then my stomach rumbled. I clutched my belly. "What was that? I feel so weak and a little nauseous. Why?"

The spell was finally broken, and Bria laughed. "You're hungry. Probably dehydrated, too. Don't move. I'll get everything we need."

Moments later, I had a sandwich in one hand and a glass of water in the other. I took a bite of the ham and cheese. "Whoa, this feels weird," I said as I chewed. Swallowing the lump of food felt foreign and I almost gagged.

"No doubt, it will take you time to get used to being alive again. Go slow with the food. You don't want to choke or throw it up."

That thought did not appeal to me, so I took small bites, chewing slowly.

Bria cut off the bottom half of my pants to fix up my leg. She cleaned it with antiseptic, causing me to yelp in pain, then pulled the torn skin back together, securing it with butterfly bandages. Lastly, she wrapped the area with gauze.

"There. Be careful with it for the next few days. We don't want it to re-open. You'll also need to keep it clean and change the dressing." She paused, packing up the first aid supplies. "This is going to be a hard transition for you. You've been immortal, practically indestructible, for a long time. You'll have to take care now, to preserve yourself through to old age."

Old age. I thought of the man in the car. It was nearly impossible to imagine, but age was something which was inevitable for me now. I felt momentarily afraid. Afraid of my frail body, afraid of death. Then, Bria sat alongside me on the sofa. She wiped my face gently with a damp cloth. For her, I would be happy to endure all this and more.

CHAPTER TWENTY

I slept a strange sleep. I was used to blacking out. Restlessness was unknown to me; waking, then sleeping in starts and stops. Around four p.m., I had fallen asleep, my physical body exhausted. When I woke for what seemed the fourth time, it was dark. The shape of Selene stood over me.

"I'll meet you downstairs," I said, moving my tongue across the front of my teeth. I needed to brush them and use the restroom, urgently. Would there be any reprieve from the needs of this human body? After only a few hours, I was already tired of it.

The bathroom light flickered on, temporarily blinding me. Looking into the mirror, I passed a hand over blond stubble. Shaving was something else I would have to learn how to do. Maybe I would get lucky, finding out Bria loved a man with a beard.

I took care of my business and then joined my sister downstairs. I sat, still weary. Brushing my teeth for the first time ever, I drew blood and tasted the iron of it on my tongue. It was no longer appetizing. The smell of coffee and food cooking set my stomach to rumbling again. "Does it ever end?" I whined.

"Bria is making you some eggs and toast." Selene

watched me for a second. With a slow shake of her head, she said, "I can't believe it. She told me everything when I woke. Still, it's unbelievable, Caesarion, really. I didn't even notice the amulet was missing last night, that's how preoccupied I was. I understand why you did it. But you should have spoken with me first. I'm sure we could have figured out another way."

"There was no other way, Selene. This was it. I couldn't take the chance you would make me back out of it." I felt so tired, like I could sleep for another eight hours straight.

She sighed. "Well, I could always re-work the change. If you want your immortality back, that is." She glanced toward the kitchen. Bria was singing a song as she prepared a meal for me.

I must admit, the thought of being immortal again was fleetingly appealing. Frankly, the human body was disgusting.

"I can't believe I'm going to say this, but no thank you. I have found a new life; a new purpose which begins and ends with the redhead."

Selene nodded her head, closing her eyes for one beat. "I figured as much. I hope the two of you will be truly happy."

I looked at my sister. "That sounds like you won't be around."

"I'll be around, here and there. But there are other people in need in the world. More demons to put down." Selene crossed her legs, sitting back. This was the most relaxed I had ever seen her.

My leg throbbed. Reaching down, I massaged my calf muscle, careful to avoid the cut.

"I can help you with that, at least." Selene held out her hand, into which I gladly lifted my leg. She gently unwrapped the bandage, then bit daintily into her finger, smearing the healing blood over the wound. Relief washed through me as it healed.

"Thank you." I took a deep breath. "Just because I'm

human now doesn't mean I can't help, you know."

"I know. You need to take some time. Get to know your body and how it works. Get to know Bria. She needs a break, too. Take a vacation, a good long one. Then you can join me. In the meantime, I'd like you to have the house. You can see to the repairs." She looked at the still boarded-up window.

"I'd love to. We may even keep the flowery furnishings."

She laughed as she got to her feet. "Hug your sister goodbye. I hate to run so quickly, but I've gotten wind of some trouble in Romania."

I enveloped her in my arms, closing my eyes to breathe in her scent. I never wanted to forget this moment. Selene left me to take her leave of Bria. I was about to settle back into the chair when there was a soft knock on the door.

There hadn't been any visitors to the cottage during my stay, so I went to the door with some trepidation. No longer would my vampiric senses alert me to danger. I peered through the peephole. Imagine my astonishment to see Millicent standing outside on the stoop. She appeared to be alone.

Dumbfounded, I stood there, watching her through the tiny window for several seconds. She crossed her arms in front of her chest. "I know you're there, Alexandre. Are you going to make me stand out here all night?"

I pulled the door open to reveal myself standing mute in the doorway. Mills raised her eyebrows. "Never have I known you to be speechless. A lot has changed, hasn't it? Your clothes, for one."

"What do you mean?" I looked down at my plaid shirt. But she was talking about more than my new fashion sense. "You know what's happened?" Of course, she knew. She could smell the human on me.

"Per your note, I know you are no longer calling yourself Alexandre. I also know you're human, if that's what you mean." Millicent looked the same as always in her skinny jeans, blousy top, and sky-high designer heels, except for one thing; she was happy. I could see it written clearly on her face.

"Let's take a walk." I stepped out next to her, pulling the door shut behind me. I wasn't sure if introducing her to my sister and Bria was in my best interest.

"Fine. Let's start with how you managed to become human. Are you okay? I've no idea why I even care." She shoved her hands inside the pockets of her jeans as we walked side by side down the walk.

I stared straight ahead as we strolled, unsure of whether I would make her uncomfortable by looking at her. "I'm rather surprised by that myself. It's all a long story. The short version is, my sister located me, sent her friend to bring me here to help them fight a god of death called Balor, along with some other demons. To seal the demon portal, called the veil, I sacrificed my immortality. So, now I'm human and I'm fine…other than being grossed out by my body."

"Got it. Makes perfect sense." She put her hand on my arm, pulling me to a stop. "Alexandre are you really okay?"

"I am. Honestly, I'm touched that you care. You shouldn't." I paused, letting my words sit between us for a moment. "How did you know…about the immortality? Did you feel it?"

She smirked. "We felt it. It was strange, there's no doubt about it. Annie and I were sitting on my back verandah, before dawn. Suddenly, we felt dizzy. I stayed in my seat. But Annie was so startled she stood, only to promptly fall over. It passed within seconds, but we were both left with this feeling of loss. I thought at the time you were dead. When we woke this evening, I decided to reach out my mind to make sure. It was then I felt you. Not only could I feel your consciousness, I could feel your humanity. I had to come and see for myself."

"What about Annie?"

She tossed her head to the side. "She's close by. She wanted to come with me but didn't want to see you. Maybe in time she will."

I nodded, sadly. It was miracle enough to see Millicent standing before me. "Please know how very sorry I am for everything, Mills."

She held up her hand. "I know. We needn't say any more about the past. Do you want this? To remain human?"

"I do. I have someone in my life. Someone who means everything. I couldn't have her as I was."

"I understand. If you need me, you know where to find me." She paused, a speck of red forming in the corner of her eye. The blood was blinked away. "What's with the name? Are you that Caesarion?"

I grinned and spread my hands. "I am. Although, now I'm thinking another name change may be in order, as it's now only associated with giving birth."

She laughed, shaking her head. "You always said your story wasn't worth talking about. Seriously? You win as having the most interesting origin of the three of us. I may need to hear it all someday."

"I know that now. I can't explain, except to say I was in denial for a long time. And I'll tell you everything, all you need to say is when."

"You're on. I guess I get the denial thing. Well, Annie had you pegged for Caesar, all along. Maybe that's what you should call yourself." She half-turned her head as if to listen to someone behind her. "I have to ask; there was never anything *mysterious* about us, other than the obvious, was there?"

"No. The only mystery about what we are was how I tried so hard to keep you by my side."

She turned her head, seemed to consider something, then leaned forward to kiss me on the cheek. "Goodbye, Alexandre. I'm sorry, but that's who you'll always be to me. I wish you happiness, I truly do."

"And happiness to you, my dear. Forever."

I watched her as she turned to walk slowly down the center of the lane.

"Tell my other kid the same," I called after her. She raised a hand in farewell, as I had done not long ago. How quickly life could change.

"Who was that?" Bria was waiting for me at the breakfast nook.

After kissing her forehead, I sat down before a plate brimming with scrambled eggs and piled with four slices of toast. My stomach growled audibly.

"That was Millicent the Marchioness," I said, starvation forcing me to dig into my plate. "Thank you for this. Is Selene gone?" I asked before stuffing a forkful of eggs in my mouth.

"She left out the back. Said she didn't want to disturb you and your friend. Although, I have a feeling she kept an eye on you before splitting. Everything okay?"

I swallowed my food as I grasped Bria's hand. I slid off her Claddagh ring, flipped it right side up, and moved it back into place. "More than okay. I've said goodbye to the past. Now I want to say hello to the future. I'm hoping that future includes you."

Her hand was as warm and soft as her smile. "I was wrong about you, you know. You did become the hero. And I'm all yours, for as long as you'd like me."

"Forever is a good start. When I count my blessings, I count you twice." I would have to memorize more proverbs before long. Bria smiled. "Selene left us the house. We can stay here or go anywhere else you want. My Irish queen will only live in the very lap of luxury."

She giggled. "I wouldn't know what to do with luxury. This house suits me fine, although I would like to travel."

I was looking forward to staying put, but if Bria wanted to travel, I wouldn't deny her request. "Any ideas?"

"A few. How about Egypt? Then Rome?"

I looked up from my plate. "That's a wonderful idea." I thought of my mother's palace and the statue of Isis from my childhood. "Perhaps the local archaeologists would like help locating a few things."

For the first time in 2,000 years, the future seemed so very bright. I couldn't help but picture myself as an old man, seated next to my love, grandchildren on our laps. I didn't know to whom I owed this second chance. I was grateful, and I would never take it for granted.

A.D. BRAZEAU

SNEAK PEEK AT BOOK FOUR IN THE IMMORTAL KINDRED SERIES... GODDESS OF THE MOON

Before I could pick up the first trunk, I heard it. The dull sound of cloven feet pawing at the soft grass. Not a tone a mortal could hear, but for me, the scraping was as clear as a bell. The sound barely preceded the smell. Demons typically had some sort of pungent, unpleasant odor. This guy was no different. He smelled of days' old refuse rotting in the sun.

I scrunched up my nose, releasing my tote which contained my laptop, letting it fall without grace to the earth. It was a good thing I paid extra for the durable case. If I was reading the situation correctly, the creature had me in its sights and would charge at any moment.

I knew what it was before I saw it, but this was not one of the creatures I had been hired to vanquish. The martolea were deceptive shapeshifters who could change their form at will. This one chose the form of a medium-size hound, as they most often did. Their diminutive size would lead one to believe they couldn't possibly be much of a threat. But, as with a vicious dog, these guys were deadly and strong.

Available Now!

BOOK ONE OF THE IMMORTAL KINDRED SERIES

True love never dies.

For Millicent, a once French noblewoman turned immortal vampire, forever is a long time to live in despair. The love of her life is murdered the night she becomes immortal. Millicent spends her endless night in a melancholy which never ends. Two hundred forty years later, she locks eyes with an English actor, who happens to look exactly like her long dead love.

Sadness turns to happiness as Millicent and Jack find passion in each other's arms. Their fling quickly turns serious as Millicent finds happiness once again— and possibly her one true love.

However, their relationship becomes complicated by her own uncertainty, Jack's mortality, and the other man in Millicent's life, Alexandre, her maker and companion. When Alexandre puts his foot down, Millicent must decide if she's going to continue to be led by others or take the reins and drive the outcome of her life.

Deepest Midnight is set in modern day Savannah, Ga with occasional glimpses back to 18th century France. This is the first book in The Immortal Kindred Series.

Available at all major book retailers

BOOK TWO OF THE IMMORTAL KINDRED SERIES

Always and Forever

Annie is a Culper Spy captured by Hessian soldiers. Powerful and mysterious Captain Thayer Emmerich takes mercy and releases her. Annie is inexplicably drawn to the handsome German, but she hates the feeling of powerlessness the enemy has left her with. Annie would give anything to be stronger.

One evening at the famous Green Dragon Tavern, Annie befriends the ethereal Millicent. Soon after meeting Millicent, Annie discovers her secret--her new friend isn't human. Millicent introduces Annie to her maker, Alexandre, and Annie joins their preternatural family.

Annie finally has the strength and freedom she needs to aid the revolution and see Thayer, once again.

The two discover a passion neither has known before. But, too many complications exist for the pair to find happily ever after. Not only are they fighting on opposite sides of the war, the evil Emilia Romanov has plans for Thayer that do not include a love affair.

Rebel Heart is set in 18th century Boston and Savannah, as well as modern day Germany and France. This is the second book in The Immortal Kindred Series.

Available at all major book retailers

ABOUT THE AUTHOR

A.D. Brazeau is an award-winning author who writes what she loves. From dark and fantastical fairytale retellings to quirky romance, and everything in between, she loves nothing more than to immerse herself in new worlds. A.D. Brazeau is a book-obsessed wife, mother, and dog lover, who grew up surrounded by stories. Not much has changed. A.D. is from Colorado Springs, Co, and currently resides in Orange County, Ca.